Having A Lover Like Sean
Was Really A Slippery Slope.

Georgia wasn't interested in trusting another man. Giving her heart over to him. Giving him the chance to crush her again. Sure, Sean was nothing like her ex, but he was still *male*.

"What do you say, Georgia?" he asked, reaching down to take her hands in his and give them a squeeze. "Will you pretend marry me?"

She couldn't think. Not with him holding on to her. Not with his eyes staring into hers. Not with the heat of him reaching for her, promising even more heat if she let him get any closer. And if she did that, she would agree to anything, because the man could have her half out of her mind in seconds, she well knew.

With him holding on to her, the beat of his heart beneath her ear, Georgia was tempted to do all sorts of things, so she looked away from him, out the window to the rain-drenched evening. Lamps lining the drive shone like diamonds in the gray. But the darkness and the incessant rain couldn't disguise the beauty that was Ireland.

Just as, she thought, looking up at Sean, a lie couldn't hide what was already between the two of them. She didn't know where it was going, but she had a feeling the ride was going to be much bumpier than she had planned.

Dear Reader,

As most of you know, I *love* Ireland. The gorgeous countryside, the incredible views everywhere you look and especially, the warm generosity of the Irish people.

The village of Dunley, where this story is set, is fictional, but I used elements of the many different villages I've stayed in to create the town itself and its citizens.

In the first book of my Irish duet, *Up Close and Personal,* you met Ronan Connolly and Laura Page, the woman who knocked his feet out from under him.

In *An Outrageous Proposal* you'll find the story of Ronan's cousin Sean Connolly and Georgia Page, Laura's sister.

These two were so much fun to write about. Sean's life is just as he wants it, and to make sure nothing changes he's willing to do whatever he has to. Georgia, on the other hand, is desperate to make changes in her life.

When these two collide, sparks fly and no one's life will ever be the same.

You'll also find a sprinkling of Gaelic in this book—a good friend of mine provided the translations. But if I've made mistakes, they're mine alone.

Thank you all so much for your continued support and the wonderful letters you write. I'm delighted to be able to spend my days writing stories for Harlequin Desire, and it's a pleasure for me to hear that you enjoy reading them!

You can visit me on Facebook, or stop in at my website, www.maureenchild.com.

Happy reading!

Maureen

MAUREEN CHILD

AN OUTRAGEOUS PROPOSAL

HARLEQUIN®

entertain, enrich, inspire™

Recycling programs
for this product may
not exist in your area.

ISBN-13: 978-0-373-73204-3

AN OUTRAGEOUS PROPOSAL

Books by Maureen Child

Harlequin Desire

Other titles by this author
available in ebook format.

Silhouette Desire

MAUREEN CHILD

is a California native who loves to travel. Every chance they get, she and her husband are taking off on another research trip. An author of more than sixty books, Maureen loves a happy ending and still swears that she has the best job in the world. She lives in Southern California with her husband, two children and a golden retriever with delusions of grandeur. Visit Maureen's website, www.maureenchild.com.

For two wonderful writers
who are fabulous friends,
Kate Carlisle and Jennifer Lyon.
Thank you both for always being there.

One

"**F**or the love of all that's holy, *don't push!*" Sean Connolly kept one wary eye on the rearview mirror and the other on the curving road stretching out in front of him. Why the hell was *he* the designated driver to the hospital?

"Just mind the road and drive, Sean," his cousin Ronan complained from the backseat. He had one arm around his hugely pregnant wife, drawing her toward him despite the seat belts.

"He's right," Georgia Page said from the passenger seat. "Just drive, Sean." She half turned to look into the back. "Hang on, Laura," she told her sister. "We'll be there soon."

"You can all relax, you know," Laura countered. "I'm not giving birth in the car."

"Please, God," Sean muttered and gave the car more gas.

Never before in his life had he had reason to curse the

narrow, winding roads of his native Ireland. But tonight, all he wanted was about thirty kilometers of smooth high-way to get them all to the hospital in Westport.

"You're not helping," Georgia muttered with a quick look at him.

"I'm driving," he told her and chanced another look into the rearview mirror just in time to see Laura's fea-tures twist in pain.

She moaned, and Sean gritted his teeth. The normal sense of panic a man felt around a woman in labor was heightened by the fact that his cousin was half excited and half mad with worry for the wife he doted on. A part of Sean envied Ronan even while the larger part of him was standing back and muttering, *Aye, Ronan, bet-ter you than me.*

Funny how complicated a man's life could get when he wasn't even paying attention to it. A year or so ago, he and his cousin Ronan were happily single, each of them with an eye toward remaining that way. Now, Ronan was married, about to be a father, and Sean was as involved in the coming birth of the next generation of Connollys as he could be. He and Ronan lived only minutes apart, and the two of them had grown up more brothers than cousins.

"Can't you go any faster?" Georgia whispered, lean-ing in toward him.

Then there was Laura's sister. Georgia was a smart, slightly cynical, beautiful woman who engaged Sean's brain even while she attracted him on a much more basic level. So far, he'd kept his distance, though. Getting in-volved with Georgia Page would only complicate things. What with her sister married to his cousin, and Ronan suddenly becoming insanely protective about the women he claimed were in "his charge."

Damned old-fashioned for a man who had spent most

of his adult years mowing through legions of adoring females.

Still, Sean was glad to have Georgia along. For the sanity she provided, if nothing else. Georgia and Sean would at least have each other to turn to during all of this, and he was grateful for it.

Sean gave her a quick glance and kept his voice low. "I go much faster on these roads at night, we'll *all* need a room in hospital."

"Right." Georgia's gaze fixed on the road ahead, and she leaned forward as if trying to make the car speed up through sheer force of will.

Well, Sean told himself, if anyone could pull that off, it would be Georgia Page. In the light from the dashboard, her dark blue eyes looked fathomless and her honey-colored hair looked more red than blond.

He'd first met her at Ronan and Laura's wedding a year or so ago, but with her many trips to Ireland to visit her sister, he'd come to know Georgia and he liked her. He liked her quick wit, her sarcasm and her sense of family loyalty—which he shared.

All around them, the darkness was complete, the head-lights of his car illuminating the narrow track winding out in front of them. This far from the city, it was mainly farmland stretching out behind the high, thick hedges that lined the road. The occasional lighted window in a farm-house stood out like beacons, urging them on.

At last, a distant glow appeared and Sean knew it was the lights of Westport, staining the night sky. They were close, and he took his first easy breath in what felt like hours.

"Nearly there," he announced, and glanced at Georgia. She gave him a quick grin, and he felt the solid punch of it.

From the backseat, Laura cried out and just like that, Sean's relief was cut short. They weren't safe yet. Focusing on the task at hand, he pushed his car as fast as he dared.

What felt like days—and was in reality only hours and hours later—Sean and Georgia walked out of the hospital like survivors of a grueling battle.

"God," Sean said, as they stepped into the soft rain of an Irish afternoon in winter. The wind blew like ice, and the rain fell from clouds that looked close enough to touch. He tipped his face back and stared up into the gray. It was good to be outside, away from the sounds and smells of the hospital. Even better to know that the latest Connolly had arrived safely.

"That was the longest night and day of my life, I think," he said with feeling.

"Mine, too," Georgia agreed, shrugging deeper into the navy blue coat she wore. "But it was worth it."

He looked over at her. "Oh, aye, it was indeed. She's a beauty."

"She is, isn't she?" Georgia grinned. "Fiona Connolly. It's a good name. Beautiful, but strong, too."

"It is, and by the look of her, she's already got her da wrapped around her tiny fingers." He shook his head as he remembered the expression on his cousin's face as Ronan held his new daughter for the first time. Almost enough to make a jaded man believe in—never mind.

"I'm exhausted and energized all at the same time."

"Me, as well," Sean agreed, happy to steer his mind away from dangerous territory. "Feel as though I've been running a marathon."

"And all we did was wait."

"I think the waiting is the hardest thing of all."

Georgia laughed. "And I think Laura would disagree."

Ruefully, he nodded. "You've a point there."

Georgia sighed, stepped up to Sean and threaded her arm through his. "Ronan will be a great father. And Laura…she wanted this so much." She sniffed and swiped her fingers under her eyes.

"No more crying," Sean said, giving her arm a squeeze. "Already I feel as though I've been riding a tide of tears all day. Between the new mother and father and you, it's been weepy eyes and sniffles for hours."

"I saw your eyes get a little misty, too, tough guy."

"Aye, well, we Irish are a sentimental lot," he admitted, then started for the car park, Georgia's arm still tucked through his.

"It's one of the things I like best about you—"

He gave her a look.

"—the Irish in general, I mean," she qualified.

"Ah, well then." He smiled to himself at her backtracking. It was a lovely afternoon. Soft rain, cold wind and new life wailing in the hospital behind them. "You've been to Ireland so often in the last year, you're very nearly an honorary Irishman yourself, aren't you?"

"I've been thinking about that," she admitted. They walked up to his car, and Sean hit the unlock button on his keypad.

"What's that then?" he asked, as he opened the passenger door for her and held it, waiting. Fatigue clawed at him, but just beneath that was a buoyant feeling that had him smile at the woman looking up at him.

"About being an honorary Irishman. Or at least," she said, looking around her at the car park, the hospital and the city beyond, "moving here. Permanently."

"Really?" Intrigued, he leaned his forearms on the top

of the door. "And what's brought this on then? Is it your brand-new niece?"

She shrugged. "Partly, sure. But mostly, it's this country. It's gorgeous and friendly, and I've really come to love being here."

"Does Laura know about this?"

"Not yet," she admitted, and shifted her gaze back to him. "So don't say anything. She's got enough on her mind at the moment."

"True enough," he said. "But I'm thinking she'd be pleased to have her sister so close."

She flashed him a brilliant smile then slid into her seat. As Sean closed the door after her and walked around the car, he was forced to admit that *he* wouldn't mind having Georgia close, either.

A half hour later, Georgia opened the door to Laura and Ronan's expansive stone manor house and looked back over her shoulder at Sean. "Want to come in for a drink?"

"I think we've earned one," he said, stepping inside and closing the door behind him. "Or even a dozen."

She laughed and it felt good. Heck, *she* felt good. Her sister was a mother, and Georgia was so glad she had made the decision to come to Ireland to be present for the baby's birth. She hated to think about what it would have been like, being a half a world away right now.

"Ronan's housekeeper, Patsy, is off in Dublin visiting her daughter Sinead," Georgia reminded him. "So we're on our own for food."

"It's not food I want at the moment anyway," Sean told her.

Was he flirting with her? Georgia wondered, then

dismissed the notion. She shook her head and reminded herself that they were here for a drink. Or several.

As he spoke, a long, ululating howl erupted from deep within the house. Georgia actually jumped at the sound and then laughed. "With the rain, the dogs have probably let themselves into the kitchen."

"Probably hungry now, too," Sean said, and walked beside her toward the back of the house.

Georgia knew her sister's house as if it were her own. Whenever she was in Ireland, she stayed here at the manor, since it was so huge they could comfortably hold a family reunion for a hundred. She opened the door into a sprawling kitchen with top-of-the-line appliances and what looked like miles of granite countertops. Everything was tidy—but for the two dogs scrambling toward her for some attention.

Deidre was a big, clumsy English sheepdog with so much hair over her eyes, it was a wonder she didn't walk into walls. And Beast—huge, homely—the best that could be said about him was what he lacked in beauty he made up for in heart. Since Beast reached her first, Georgia scratched behind his ears and sent the big dog into quivers of delight. Deidre was right behind him, nudging her mate out of her way.

"Okay then, food for the dogs, then drinks for us," Georgia announced.

"Already on it," Sean assured her, making his way to the wide pantry, stepping over and around Beast as the dog wound his way in and out of Sean's feet.

Within a few minutes, they had the dogs fed and watered and then left them there, sleeping on their beds in front of the now cold kitchen hearth. Cuddled up together, the dogs looked snug and happy.

Then Georgia led the way back down the hall, the

short heels of her shoes clicking against the wood floor. At the door to the parlor, Sean asked, "So, Patsy's in Dublin with her daughter. Sinead's doing well then, with her new family?"

"According to Patsy, everything's great," Georgia said.

Laura had told her the whole story of the pregnant Sinead marrying in a hurry. Sinead was now the mother of an infant son and her new husband was, at the moment, making a demo CD. He and his friends played traditional Irish music and, thanks to Ronan's influence with a recording company, had a real chance to do something with it. "She misses Sinead living close by, but once they get the demo done, they'll all be coming back to Dunley."

"Home does draw a body back no matter how far you intend to roam," Sean mused, as he followed her into the front parlor. "And yet, you're thinking of leaving your home to make a new one."

"I guess I am."

Hearing him say it aloud made the whole idea seem more real than it had in the past week or so that it had been floating around in her mind. But it also felt…right. Okay, scary, but good. After all, it wasn't as if she was giving up a lot. And the plus side was, she could leave behind all of the tension and bad memories of a marriage that had dissolved so abruptly.

Moving to Ireland was a big change, she knew. But wasn't change a good thing? Shake up your life from time to time just to keep it interesting?

At that thought, she smiled to herself. Interesting. Moving to a different country. Leaving the familiar to go to the…okay, also familiar. Since Laura had married Ronan and moved to Ireland, Georgia had made the long trek to visit four times. And each time she came, it was harder to leave. To go back to her empty condo in Huntington Beach, California. To sit at her desk, alone in the real estate office she and Laura had opened together.

Not that she was feeling sorry for herself—she wasn't. But she had started thinking that maybe there was more to life than sitting behind a desk hoping to sell a house.

In the parlor, Georgia paused, as she always did, just to enjoy the beauty of the room. A white-tiled hearth, cold now, but stacked with kindling that Sean was already working to light against the chill gloom of the day. Pale green walls dotted with seascapes and oversize couches facing each other across a low table that held a Waterford crystal bowl filled with late chrysanthemums in tones of russet and gold. The wide front windows looked out over a sweep of lawn that was drenched with the rain still falling softly against the glass.

When he had the fire going to his satisfaction, Sean stood up and brushed his palms together, then moved to the spindle table in the corner that held a collection of crystal decanters. Ignoring them, he bent to the small refrigerator tucked into the corner behind the table.

"Now, about that celebratory drink," he muttered.

Georgia smiled and joined him at the table, leaning her palms on the glossy top as she watched him open the fridge. "We earned it all right, but I wouldn't have missed it. The worry, the panic—" She was still smiling as he glanced up at her. "And I was seriously panicked. It was hard knowing Laura was in pain and not being able to do anything about it."

"Would it make me seem less manly to you if I admitted to sheer terror?" he asked, as he reached into the refrigerator.

"Your manhood is safe," Georgia assured him.

In fact, she had never known a man who needed to worry less about his manhood than Sean Connolly. He was gorgeous, charming and oozed sex appeal. Good thing, she thought, that she was immune. Well, nearly.

Even she, a woman who knew better, had been tempted by Sean's charms. Of course, it would be much better—safer—to keep him in the "friend" zone. Starting up anything with him would not only be dangerous but awkward, as well. Since her sister was married to his cousin, any kind of turmoil between them could start a family war.

And there was *always* turmoil when a man was involved, she thought with an inner sigh. But she'd learned her lesson there. She could enjoy Sean's company without letting herself get...involved. Her gaze skimmed over his tall, nicely packed yet lanky body, and something inside her sizzled like a trapped flame struggling to grow into a bonfire. She so didn't need that.

Nope, she told herself, just enjoy looking at him and keep your hormones on a tight leash. When he sent her a quick wink and a wild grin, Georgia amended that last thought to a tight, *short,* leash.

To divert herself from her own thoughts, Georgia sighed and asked, "Isn't she beautiful? The baby?"

"She is indeed," Sean agreed, pulling a bottle of champagne from the fridge and holding it aloft like a hard-won trophy. "And she has a clever father, as well. Our Ronan's stocked the fridge with not one but three bottles of champagne, bless him."

"Very thoughtful," she agreed.

He grabbed two crystal flutes from the shelf behind the bar, then set them down on the table and worked at the champagne wire and cork. "Did you get hold of your parents with the news?"

"I did," Georgia said, remembering how her mother had cried over the phone hearing the news about her first grandchild. "I called from Laura's room when you took Ronan down to buy flowers. Laura got to talk to them and they heard the baby cry." She smiled. "Mom cried along with her. Ronan's already promised to fly them in whenever they're ready."

"That's lovely then." The cork popped with a cheerful sound, and Sean poured out two glasses. Bubbling froth filled the flutes, looking like liquid sunshine. "So, champagne?"

"Absolutely."

She took a glass and paused when Sean said, "To Fiona Connolly. May her life be long and happy. May she be a stranger to sorrow and a friend to joy."

The sting of tears burned Georgia's eyes. Shaking her head, she took a sip of champagne and said, "That was beautiful, Sean."

He gave her a grin, then took her free hand in his and led her over to one of the sofas. There, he sat her down and then went back to the bar for the bottle of champagne. He set it on the table in front of them, then took a seat beside Georgia on the couch.

"A hell of a day all in all, wouldn't you say?"

"It was," she agreed, then amended, *"is."* Another sip of champagne and she added, "I'm tired, but I don't think I could close my eyes, you know? Too much left-over adrenaline pumping away inside."

"I feel the same," he told her, "so it's lucky we can keep each other company."

"Yeah, I guess it is," Georgia agreed. Kicking her shoes off, she drew her feet up onto the sofa and idly rubbed her arches.

The snap and hiss of the fire along with the patter of rain on the window made for a cozy scene. Taking a sip of her champagne, she let her head fall back against the couch.

"So," Sean said a moment or two later, "tell me about this plan of yours to move to Ireland."

She lifted her head to look at him. His brown hair was tousled, his brown eyes tired but interested and the half smile on his face could have tempted a saint. Georgia took another sip of champagne, hoping the icy liquor would dampen the heat beginning to build inside.

"I've been thinking about it for a while," she admitted, her voice soft. "Actually since my last visit. When I left for home, I remember sitting on the airplane as it was taxiing and wondering why I was leaving."

He nodded as if he understood completely, and that settled her enough to continue.

"I mean, you should be happy to go home after a trip, right?" She asked the question more of herself than of Sean and answered it the same way. "Looking forward to going back to your routine. Your everyday life. But I wasn't. There was just this niggling sense of disappointment that seemed to get bigger the closer I got to home."

"Maybe some of that was just because you were leaving your sister," he said quietly.

"Probably," she admitted with a nod and another sip of champagne. "I mean, Laura's more than my sister, she's my best friend." Looking at him, she gave him a small smile. "I really miss having her around, you know?"

"I do," he said, reaching for the champagne, then topping off their glasses. "When Ronan was in California, I found I missed going to the pub with him. I missed the laughter. And the arguments." He grinned. "Though if you repeat any of this, I'll deny it to my last breath."

"Oh, understood," she replied with a laugh. "Anyway, I got home, went to our—*my*—real estate office and stared out the front window. Waiting for clients to call or come in is a long, boring process." She stared down into her champagne. "And while I was staring out that window, watching the world go by, I realized that everyone outside the glass was doing what they wanted to do. Everyone but me."

"I thought you enjoyed selling real estate," Sean said. "The way Laura tells it, the two of you were just beginning to build the business."

"We were," she agreed. "But it wasn't what either of us wanted. Isn't that ridiculous?" Georgia shifted on the couch, half turning to face Sean more fully.

Wow, she thought, *he really is gorgeous.*

She blinked, then looked at the champagne suspiciously. Maybe the bubbles were infiltrating her mind, making her more susceptible to the Connolly charm and good looks. But no, she decided a moment later, she'd always been susceptible. Just able to resist. But now...

Georgia cleared her throat and banished her wayward thoughts. What had she been saying? Oh, yeah.

"I mean, think about it. Laura's an artist, and I was an interior designer once upon a time. And yet there we were, building a business neither of us was really interested in."

"Why is that?" He watched her out of those beautiful brown eyes and seemed genuinely curious. "Why would you put so much of yourselves into a thing you'd no interest in?"

"Well, that's the question, isn't it?" she asked, gesturing with her glass and cringing a little when the champagne slopped over the brim. To help fix that situation, she sipped the contents down a bit lower. "It started simply enough," she continued. "Laura couldn't make a living painting, so she took classes and became a real estate agent because she'd rather be her own boss, you know?"

"I do," he said with a knowing nod.

Of course he understood that part, Georgia thought. As the owner of Irish Air, a huge and growing airline, Sean made his own rules. Sure, their situations were wildly different, but he would still get the feeling of being answerable only to oneself.

"Then my marriage dissolved," she said, the words still tasting a little bitter. Georgia was mostly over it all, since it had been a few years now, but if she allowed herself to remember... "I moved out to live with Laura, and rather than try to build up a brand-new business of my own—and let's face it, in California, you practically stumble across an interior designer every few steps, so they didn't really need another one—I took classes and the two of us opened our own company."

Shaking her head, she drank more of the champagne and sighed. "So basically, we both backed into a business we didn't really want, but couldn't think of a way to get out of. Does that make sense?"

"Completely," Sean told her. "What it comes down to is, you weren't happy."

"*Exactly.*" She took a deep breath and let it go again. What was it about him? she wondered. So easy to talk to. So nice to look at, a tiny voice added from the back of her mind. Those eyes of his seemed to look deep inside her, while the lilt of Ireland sang in his voice. A heady combination, she warned herself. "I wasn't happy. And, since I'm free and on my own, why shouldn't I move to Ireland? Be closer to my sister? Live in a place I've come to love?"

"No reason a'tall," he assured her companionably. Picking up the champagne bottle he refilled both of their glasses again, and Georgia nodded her thanks. "So, I'm guessing you won't be after selling real estate here then?"

"No, thank you," she said on a sigh. God, it felt wonderful to know that soon she wouldn't have to deal with recalcitrant sellers and pushy buyers. When people came to her for design work, they would be buying her talent, not whatever house happened to be on the market.

"I'm going to open my own design shop. Of course, I'll have to check everything out first, see what I have to do to get a business license in Ireland and to have my interior design credentials checked. And I'll have to have a house…"

"You could always stay here," he said with a shrug. "I'm sure Ronan and Laura would love to have you here with them, and God knows the place is big enough…"

"It is that," she mused, shifting her gaze around the parlor of the luxurious manor house. In fact, the lovely old house was probably big enough for two or three families. "But I'd rather have a home of my own. My own place, not too far. I'm thinking of opening my shop in Dunley…"

Sean choked on a sip of champagne, then laughed a second later. "*Dunley?* You want to open a design shop in the *village?*"

Irritated, she scowled at him. And he'd been doing so nicely on the understanding thing, too. "What's wrong with that?"

"Well, let's just say I can't see Danny Muldoon hiring you to give the Pennywhistle pub a makeover anytime soon."

"Funny," she muttered.

"Ah now," Sean said, smile still firmly in place, "don't get yourself in a twist. I'm only saying that perhaps the city might be a better spot for a design shop."

Still frowning, she gave him a regal half nod. "Maybe. But Dunley is about halfway between Galway and Westport—two big cities, you'll agree—"

"I do."

"So, the village is centrally located, and I'd rather be in a small town than a big one anyway. And I can buy a cottage close by and walk to work. Living in the village, I'll be a part of things as I wouldn't if I lived in Galway and only visited on weekends. *And,*" she added, on a roll, "I'd be close to Laura to visit or help with the baby. Not to mention—"

"You're right, absolutely." He held up both hands, then noticed his champagne glass was nearly empty. He refilled his, and hers, and then lifted his glass in a toast. "I'm sorry I doubted you for a moment. You've thought this through."

"I really have," she said, a little mellower now, thanks not only to the wine, but to the gleam of admiration in Sean's gaze. "I want to do this. I'm *going* to do this," she added, a promise to herself and the universe at large.

"And so you will, I've no doubt," Sean told her, leaning forward. "To the start of more than *one* new life this day. I wish you happiness, Georgia, with your decision and your shop."

"Thanks," she said, clinking her glass against his, making the heavy crystal sing. "I appreciate it."

When they'd both had a sip to seal the toast, Sean mused, "So we'll be neighbors."

"We will."

"And friends."

"That, too," she agreed, feeling just a little unsettled by his steady stare and the twisting sensation in the pit of her stomach.

"And as your friend," Sean said softly, "I think I should tell you that when you're excited about something, your eyes go as dark as a twilight sky."

Two

"What?"

Sean watched the expression on her face shift from confusion to a quick flash of desire that was born and then gone again in a blink. But he'd seen it, and his response to it was immediate.

"Am I making you nervous, Georgia?"

"No," she said and he read the lie in the way she let her gaze slide from his. After taking another sip of champagne, she licked a stray drop from her lip, and Sean's insides fisted into knots.

Odd, he'd known Georgia for about a year now and though he'd been attracted, he'd never before been tempted. Now he was. Most definitely. Being here with her in the fire-lit shadows while rain pattered at the windows was, he thought, more than tempting. There was an intimacy here, two people who had shared a hellishly long day together. Now, in the quiet shadows, there was something new and…compelling rising up between them.

He knew she felt it, too, despite the wary gleam in her eyes as she watched him. Still, he wanted her breathless, not guarded, so he eased back and gave her a half smile. "I'm only saying you're a beautiful woman, Georgia."

"Hmm…" She tipped her head to one side, studying him.

"Surely it's not the first time you've heard that from a man."

"Oh, no," she answered. "Men actually chase me down the street to tell me I have twilight eyes."

He grinned. He did appreciate a quick wit. "Maybe I'm just more observant than most men."

"And maybe you're up to something," she said thoughtfully. "What is it, Sean?"

"Not a thing," he said, all innocence.

"Well, that's good." She nodded and reached down absently to rub at the arch of her foot. "I mean, we both know anything else would just be…complicated."

"Aye, it would at that," he agreed, and admitted silently that complicated might be worth it. "Your feet hurt?"

"What?" She glanced down to where her hand rubbed the arch of her right foot and smiled ruefully. "Yeah, they do."

"A long day of standing, wasn't it?"

"It was."

She sipped at her champagne and a log shifted in the fire. As the flames hissed and spat, she closed her eyes— a little dreamily, he thought, and he felt that fist inside him tighten even further. The woman was unknowingly seducing him.

Logic and a stern warning sounded out in his mind, and he firmly shut them down. There was a time for a cool head, and there was a time for finding out just where the road you found yourself on would end up. So far, he liked this particular road very much.

He set his glass on the table in front of them, then sat back and dragged her feet onto his lap. Georgia looked at him and he gave her a quick grin. "I'm offering a one-night-only special. A foot rub."

"Sean…"

He knew what she was thinking because his own mind was running along the same paths. Back up—or, stay the course and see what happened. As she tried to draw her feet away, he held them still in his lap and pushed his thumbs into her arch.

She groaned and let her head fall back and he knew he had her.

"Oh, that feels too good," she whispered, as he continued to rub and stroke her skin.

"Just enjoy it for a bit then," he murmured.

That had her lifting her head to look at him with the wariness back, glinting in those twilight depths. "What're you up to?"

"Your ankles," he said, sliding his hands higher to match his words. "Give me a minute, though, and ask again."

She laughed as he'd meant her to, and the wariness edged off a bit.

"So," she asked a moment later, "why do I rate a foot rub tonight?"

"I'm feeling generous, just becoming an uncle and all." He paused, and let that settle. Of course, he and Ronan weren't actually brothers, but they might as well have been. "Not really an uncle, but that's how it feels."

"You're an uncle," she told him. "You and Ronan are every bit as tight as Laura and I are."

"True," he murmured, and rubbed his thumb into the arches of her small, narrow feet. Her toes were painted a dark pink, and he smiled at the silver toe ring she wore on her left foot.

She sighed heavily and whispered, "Oh, my...you've got great hands."

"So I've been told," he said on a laugh. He slid his great hands a bit higher, stroking her ankles and then up along the line of her calves. Her skin was soft, smooth and warm, now that the fire had chased away the chill of the afternoon.

"Maybe it's the champagne talking," she said softly, "but what you're doing feels way too good."

"'Tisn't the champagne," he told her, meeting her eyes when she looked at him. "We've not had enough yet to blur the lines between us."

"Then it's the fire," she whispered, "and the rain outside sealing us into this pretty room together."

"Could be," he allowed, sliding his hands even higher now, stroking the backs of her knees and watching her eyes close as she sighed. "And it could just be that you're a lovely thing, here in the firelight, and I'm overcome."

She snorted and he grinned in response.

"Oh, yes, overcome," she said, staring into his eyes again, as if trying to see the plans he had, the plans he might come up with. "Sean Connolly, you're a man who always knows what he's doing. So answer me this. Are you trying to seduce me?"

"Ah, the shoe is on the other foot entirely, Georgia," he murmured, his fingertips moving higher still, up her thighs, inch by inch. He hadn't thought of it earlier, but now he was grateful she'd been wearing a skirt for their mad ride to the hospital. Made things so much simpler.

"Right," she said. "I'm seducing you? You're the one

giving out foot rubs that have now escalated—" her breath caught briefly before she released it on a sigh "—to *thigh* rubs."

"And do you like it?"

"I'd be a fool not to," she admitted, and he liked her even more for her straightforwardness.

"Well then..."

"But the question remains," she said, reaching down to capture one of his hands in hers, stilling his caresses. "If you're seducing me, I have to ask, why now? We've known each other for so long, Sean, and we've never—"

"True enough," he murmured, "but this is the first time we've been alone, isn't it?" He set her hand aside and continued to stroke the outsides of her thighs before slowly edging around to the inside.

She squirmed, and he went hard as stone.

"Think of it, Georgia," he continued, though his voice was strained and it felt as though there were a rock lodged in his throat. "'Tis just us here for the night. No Ronan, no Laura, no Patsy, running in and out with her tea trays. Even the dogs are in the kitchen sleeping."

Georgia laughed a little. "You're right. I don't think I've ever been in this house alone before. But..."

"No buts," he interrupted, then leaned out and picked up the champagne bottle. Refilling her glass and then his own, he set the bottle down again and lifted his glass with one hand while keeping her feet trapped in his lap with the other. "I think we need more of this, then we'll...*talk* about this some more."

"After enough champagne, we won't want to talk at all," she said, though she sipped at the wine anyway.

"And isn't that a lovely thought?" he asked, giving her a wink as he drained his glass.

She was watching him, and her eyes were filled with

the same heat that burned inside him. For the life of him, Sean couldn't figure out how he'd managed to keep his hands off of her for the past year or more. Right now, the desire leaping inside him had him hard and eager for the taste of her. The feel of her beneath his hands. He wanted to hear her sigh, hear her call his name as she erupted beneath him. Wanted to bury himself inside her heat and feel her surrounding him.

"That look in your eyes tells me exactly what you're thinking," Georgia said, and this time she took a long drink of champagne.

"And are you thinking the same?" he asked.

"I shouldn't be."

"That wasn't the question."

Never breaking her gaze from his, Georgia blew out a breath and admitted, "Okay, yes, I'm thinking the same."

"Thank the gods for that," he said, a smile curving his mouth.

She chuckled, and the sound was rich and full. "I think you've got more in common with the devils than you do with the gods."

"Isn't that a lovely thing to say then?" he quipped. Reaching out, he plucked the champagne flute from her hand and set it onto the table.

"I wasn't finished," she told him.

"We'll have more later. *After,*" he promised.

She took a deep breath and said, "This is probably a mistake, you know."

"Aye, probably is. Would you have us stop then, before we get started?" He hoped to hell she said no, because if she said yes, he'd have to leave. And right now, leaving was the very last thing he wanted to do.

"I really should say yes, because we absolutely should stop. Probably," she said quietly.

He liked the hesitation in that statement. "But?"

"But," she added, "I'm tired of being sensible. I want you to touch me, Sean. I think I've wanted that right from the beginning, but we were being too sensible for me to admit to it."

He pulled her up and over to him, settling her on his lap where she'd be sure to feel the hard length of him pressing into her bottom. "You can readily see that I feel the same."

"Yeah," she said, turning her face up to his. "I'm getting that."

"Not yet," he teased, "but you're about to."

"Promises, promises…"

"Well then, enough talking, yes?"

"Oh, yes."

He kissed her, softly at first, a brush of the lips, a connection that was as swift and sweet as innocence. It was a tease. Something short to ease them both into this new wrinkle in their relationship.

But with that first kiss, something incredible happened. Sean felt a jolt of white-hot electricity zip through him in an instant. His eyes widened as he looked at her, and he knew the surprise he read on her face was also etched on his own.

"That was… Let's just see if we can make that happen again, shall we?"

She nodded and arched into him, parting her lips for him when he kissed her, and this time Sean fed that electrical jolt that sizzled between them. He deepened the kiss, tangling his tongue with hers, pulling her closer, tighter, to him. Her arms came up around his neck and held on. She kissed him back, feverishly, as if every ounce of passion within her had been unleashed at once.

She stabbed her fingers through his hair, nails dragging along his scalp. She twisted on his lap, rubbing her behind against his erection until a groan slid from his throat. The glorious friction of her body against his would only get better, he thought, if he could just get her out of these bloody clothes.

He broke the kiss and dragged in a breath of air, hoping to steady the racing beat of his heart. It didn't help. Nothing would. Not until he'd had her, all of her. Only then would he be able to douse the fire inside. To cool the need and regain his control.

But for now, all he needed was her. Georgia Page, temptress with eyes of twilight and a mouth designed to drive a man wild.

"You've too many clothes on," he muttered, dropping his hands to the buttons on her dark blue shirt.

"You, too," she said, tugging the tail of his white, long-sleeved shirt free of the black jeans he wore. She fumbled at the buttons and then laughed at herself. "Can't get them undone, damn it."

"No need," he snapped and, gripping both sides of his shirt, ripped it open, sending small white buttons flying around the room like tiny missiles.

She laughed again and slapped both palms to his chest. At the first touch of her skin to his, Sean hissed in a breath and held it. He savored every stroke, every caress, while she explored his skin as if determined to map every inch of him.

He was willing to lie still for that exploration, too, as long as he could do the same for her. He got the last of her buttons undone and slid her shirt off her shoulders and down her arms. She helped him with it, and then her skin was bared to him, all but her lovely breasts, hidden behind the pale, sky-blue lace of her bra. His mouth went dry.

Tossing her honey-blond hair back from her face, Georgia met his gaze as she unhooked the front clasp of that bra and then slipped out of it completely. Sean's hands cupped her, his thumbs and forefingers brushing across the rigid peaks of her dark pink nipples until she sighed and cupped his hands with her own.

"You're lovely, Georgia. More lovely than I'd imagined," he whispered, then winked. "And my imagination was pretty damned good."

She grinned, then whispered, "My turn." She pushed his shirt off and skimmed her small, elegant hands slowly over his shoulders and arms, and every touch was a kiss of fire. Every caress a temptation.

He leaned over, laying her back on the sofa until she was staring up at him. Firelight played over her skin, light and shadow dancing in tandem, making her seem almost ethereal. But she was a real woman with a real need, and Sean was the man to meet it.

Deftly, he undid the waist button and the zipper of the skirt she wore, then slowly tugged the fabric down and off before tossing it to the floor. She wore a scrap of blue lace panties that were somehow even more erotic than seeing her naked would have been. Made him want to take that elastic band between his teeth and—

"Sean!" She half sat up and for a dark second or two, Sean was worried she'd changed her mind at the last. The thought of that nearly brought him to his knees.

"What is it?"

"Protection," she said. "I'm not on the pill, and I don't really travel with condoms." Worrying her bottom lip with her teeth, she blurted, "Maybe Ronan's got some old ones upstairs…"

"No need," he said and stood. "I've some in the glove box of the car."

She just looked at him. "You keep condoms in the glove compartment?"

Truthfully, he hadn't used any of the stash he kept there for emergencies in longer than he cared to admit. There hadn't been a woman for him in months. Maybe, he thought now, it was because he'd been too tangled up in thoughts of twilight eyes and kissable lips. Well, he didn't much care for the sound of that, so he told himself that maybe he'd just been too bloody busy getting his airline off the ground, so to speak.

"Pays to be prepared," was all he said.

Georgia's lips twitched. "I didn't realize Ireland *had* Boy Scouts."

"What?"

"Never mind," she whispered, lifting her hips and pulling her panties off. "Just…hurry."

"I bloody well will." He scraped one hand across his face, then turned and bolted for the front door. It cost him to leave her, even for the few moments this necessary trip would take.

He was through the front door and out to his car in a blink. He hardly felt the misting rain as it covered him in an icy, wet blanket. The night was quiet; the only light came from that of the fire within the parlor, a mere echo of light out here, battling and losing against the darkness and the rain.

He tore through the glove box, grabbed the box of condoms and slammed the door closed again. Back inside the house, he staggered to a stop on the threshold of the parlor. She'd moved from the couch, and now she lay stretched out, naked, on the rug before the fire, her head on one of the countless pillows she'd brought down there with her.

Sean's gaze moved over her in a flash and then again,

more slowly, so he could savor everything she was. Mouth dry, heartbeat hammering in his chest, he thought he'd never seen a more beautiful picture than the one she made in the firelight.

"You're wet," she whispered.

Sean shoved one hand through his rain-soaked hair, then shrugged off his shirt. "Hadn't noticed."

"Cold?" she asked, and levered herself up on one elbow to watch him.

The curve of her hip, the swell of her breasts and the heat in her eyes all came together to flash into an inferno inside him. "Cold? Not likely."

Never taking his gaze from hers, he pulled off the rest of his clothes and simply dropped them onto the colorful rug beneath his feet. He went to her, laser-focused on the woman stretched out beside him on the carpet in the firelight.

She reached up and cupped his cheek before smiling. "I thought we'd have more room down here than on the couch."

"Very sensible," he muttered, kissing her palm then dipping to claim her lips in a brief, hard kiss. "Nothing more sexy than a smart woman."

"Always nice to hear." She grinned and moved into him, pressing her mouth to his. Opening for him, welcoming the taste of him as he devoured her. Bells clanged in his mind, warning or jubilation he didn't care which.

All that mattered now was the next touch. The next taste. She filled him as he'd never been filled before and all Sean could think was *Why had it taken them so bloody long to do this?*

Then his thoughts dissolved under an onslaught of sensations that flooded his system. He tore his mouth from hers to nibble at the underside of her jaw. To drag lips and tongue along the line of her throat while she sighed with pleasure and slid her hands up and down his back.

She was soft, smooth and smelled of flowers, and every breath he took drew her deeper inside him. He lost himself in the discovery of her, sliding his palms over her curves. He took first one nipple, then the other, into his mouth, tasting, suckling, driving her sighs into desperate gasps for air. She touched him, too, sliding her hands across his back and around to his chest and then down, to his abdomen. Then further still, until she curled her fingers around his length and Sean lifted his head, looked down into her eyes and let her see what she was doing to him.

Firelight flickered, rain spattered against the windows and the wind rattled the glass.

Her breath came fast and heavy. His heart galloped in his chest. Reaching for the condoms he'd tossed to the hearth, he tore one packet open, sheathed himself, then moved to kneel between her legs.

She planted her feet and lifted her hips in invitation and Sean couldn't wait another damn minute. He needed this. Needed *her* as he'd never needed anything before.

Scooping his hands beneath her butt, he lifted her and, in one swift push, buried himself inside her.

Her head fell back, and a soft moan slid from her lips. His jaw tight, he swallowed the groan trying to escape his throat. Then she wrapped her legs around his middle, lifted her arms and drew him in deeper, closer. He bent over her and kissed her as the rhythm of this ancient, powerful dance swept them both away.

They moved together as if they'd been partners for years. Each seemed to know instinctively what would most touch, most inflame, the other. Their shadows moved on the walls and the night crowded closer as Sean pushed Georgia higher and higher.

His gaze locked with hers, he watched her eyes flash, felt her body tremble as her release exploded inside her. Lost himself in the pleasure glittering in her twilight eyes and then, finally, his control snapped completely. Taking her mouth with his, he kissed her deeply as his body shattered.

Georgia felt...fabulous.

Heat from the fire warmed her on one side, while Sean's amazing body warmed her from the other. And of the two, she preferred the heat pumping from the tall, gorgeous man laying beside her.

Turning to face him, she smiled. "That was—"

"Aye, it was," he agreed.

"Worth waiting for," she confessed.

He skimmed a palm along the curve of her hip and she shivered. "And I was just wondering why in the hell we waited as long as we did."

"Worried about complications, remember?" she asked, and only now felt the first niggling doubt about whether or not they'd done the right thing. Probably not, she mused, but it was hard to regret any of it.

"There's always complications to good sex," he said softly, "and that wasn't just good, it was—"

"Yeah," she said, "it was."

"So the question arises," he continued, smoothing his hand now across her bottom, "what do we do about this?"

She really hadn't had time to consider all the options, and Georgia was a woman who spent most of her life looking at any given situation from every angle possible. Well, until tonight anyway. Now, her brain was scrambling to come up with coherent thoughts in spite of the fact that her body was still buzzing and even now hoping for more.

Still, one thing did come to mind, though she didn't much care for it. "We could just stop whatever this is. Pretend tonight never happened and go back to the way things were."

"And is that what you really want to do?" he asked, leaning forward to plant a kiss on her mouth.

She licked her lips as if to savor the taste of him, then sighed and shook her head. "No, I really don't. But those complications will only get worse if we keep doing this."

"Life is complicated, Georgia," he said, smoothing his hand around her body to tug playfully at one nipple.

She sucked in a gulp of air and blew it out again. "True."

"And, pretending it didn't happen won't work, as every time I see you, I'll want to do this again…"

"There is that," she said, reaching out to smooth his hair back from his forehead. Heck, she *already* wanted to do it all again. Feel that moment when his body slid into hers. Experience the sensation of his body filling hers completely. That indescribable friction that only happened when sex was done really well. And this *so* had been.

His eyes in the firelight glittered as if there were sparks dancing in their depths, and Georgia knew she was a goner. At least for now, anyway. She might regret it all later, but if she did, she would still walk away with some amazing memories.

"So," he said softly, "we'll take the complications as they come and do as we choose?"

"Yes," she said after giving the thought of never being with him again no more than a moment's consideration.

"We'll take the complications. We're adults. We know what we're doing."

"We certainly seemed to a few minutes ago," he said with a teasing grin.

"Okay, then. No strings. No expectations. Just…*us*. For however long it lasts."

"Sounds good." He pushed himself to his feet and walked naked to the table where they'd abandoned their wineglasses and the now nearly empty bottle of champagne.

"What're you doing?"

He passed her the glasses as she sat up, then held the empty bottle aloft. "I'm going to open another of Ronan's fine bottles of champagne. The first we drank to our new and lovely Fiona. The second we'll drink to *us*. And the bargain we've just made."

She looked up at him, her gaze moving over every square inch of that deliciously toned and rangy body. He looked like some pagan god, doused in firelight, and her breath stuttered in her chest. She could only nod to his suggestion because her throat was so suddenly tight with need, with passion, with…other things she didn't even want to contemplate.

Sean Connolly wasn't a forever kind of man—but, Georgia reminded herself as she watched him move to the tiny refrigerator and open it, she wasn't looking for forever. She'd already tried that and had survived the crash-and-burn. Sure, he wasn't the man her ex had been. But why even go there? Why try to make more out of this than it was? Great sex didn't have to be forever.

And as a right-now kind of man, Sean was perfect.

Three

The next couple of weeks were busy.

Laura was just settling into life as a mother, and both she and Ronan looked asleep on their feet half the time. But there was happiness in the house, and Georgia was determined to find some of that happy for herself.

Sean had been a big help in navigating village society. Most of the people who lived and worked in Dunley had been there for generations. And though they might like the idea of a new shop in town, the reality of it slammed up against the whole aversion-to-change thing. Still, since Georgia was no longer a complete stranger, most of the people in town were more interested than resentful.

"A design shop, you say?"

"That's right," Georgia answered, turning to look at Maeve Carrol. At five feet two inches tall, the seventy-year-old woman had been Ronan's nanny once upon a long-ago time. Since then, she was the self-appointed chieftain of the village and kept up with everything that was happening.

Her white hair was piled at the top of her head in a lop-sided bun. Her cheeks were red from the wind, and her blue eyes were sharp enough that Georgia was willing to bet Maeve didn't miss much. Buttoned up in a Kelly green cardigan and black slacks, she looked snug, right down to the soles of her bright pink sneakers.

"And you'll draw up pictures of things to be done to peoples' homes."

"Yes, and businesses, as well," Georgia said, "just about anything. It's all about the flow of a space. Not exactly feng shui but along the same lines."

Maeve's nose twitched and a smile hovered at the corners of her mouth. "Fing Shooey—not a lot of that in the village."

Georgia smiled at Maeve's pronunciation of the design philosophy, then said, "Doesn't matter. Some will want help redecorating, and there will be customers for me in Westport and Galway…"

"True enough," Maeve allowed.

Georgia paused to take a look up and down the main street she'd come to love over the past year. There really wasn't much to the village, all in all. The main street held a few shops, the Pennywhistle pub, a grocer's, the post office and a row of two-story cottages brightly painted.

The sidewalks were swept every morning by the shop owners, and flowers spilled from pots beside every doorway. The doors were painted in brilliant colors, scarlet, blue, yellow and green, as if the bright shades could offset the ever-present gray clouds.

There were more homes, of course, some above the shops and some just outside the village proper on the narrow track that wound through the local farmers' fields.

Dunley had probably looked much the same for centuries, she thought, and liked the idea very much.

It would be good to have roots. To belong. After her divorce, Georgia had felt so…untethered. She'd lived in Laura's house, joined Laura's business. Hadn't really had something to call *hers*. This was a new beginning. A chapter in her life that she would write in her own way in her own time. It was a heady feeling.

Outside of town was a cemetery with graves dating back five hundred years or more, each of them still lovingly tended by the descendants of those who lay there. The ruins of once-grand castles stubbled the countryside and often stood side by side with the modern buildings that would never be able to match the staying power of those ancient structures.

And soon, she would be a part of it.

"It's a pretty village," Georgia said with a little sigh.

"It is at that," Maeve agreed. "We won the Tidy Town award back in '74, you know. The Mayor's ever after us to win it again."

"Tidy Town." She smiled as she repeated the words and loved the fact that soon she would be a part of the village life. She might always be called "the Yank," but it would be said with affection, she thought, and one day, everyone might even forget that Georgia Page hadn't always been there.

She hoped so, anyway. This was important to her. This life makeover. And she wanted—needed—it to work.

"You've your heart set on this place, have you?" Maeve asked.

Georgia grinned at the older woman then shifted her gaze to the empty building in front of them. It was at the end of the village itself and had been standing empty for a couple of years. The last renter had given up on making a go of it and had left for America.

"I have," Georgia said with a sharp nod for emphasis. "It's a great space, Maeve—"

"Surely a lot of it," the older woman agreed, peering through dirty windows to the interior. "Colin Ferris now, he never did have a head for business. Imagine trying to make a living selling interwebbing things in a village the size of Dunley."

Apparently Colin hadn't been able to convince the villagers that an internet café was a good idea. And there hadn't been enough of the tourist trade to tide him over.

"'Twas no surprise to me he headed off to America." She looked over at Georgia. "Seems only right that one goes and one comes, doesn't it?"

"It does." She hadn't looked at it that way before, but there was a sort of synchronicity to the whole thing. Colin left for America, and Georgia left America for Dunley.

"So you've your path laid out then?"

"What? Oh. Yes, I guess I have," Georgia said, smiling around the words. She had found the building she would rent for her business, and maybe in a couple of years, she'd be doing so well she would buy it. It was all happening, she thought with an inner grin. Her whole life was changing right before her eyes. Georgia would never again be the same woman she had been when Mike had walked out of her life, taking her self-confidence with him.

"Our Sean's been busy as well, hasn't he?" Maeve mused aloud. "Been a help to you right along?"

Cautious, Georgia slid a glance at the canny woman beside her. So far she and Sean had kept their…relationship under the radar. And in a village the size of Dunley, that had been a minor miracle. But if Maeve Carrol was paying attention, their little secret could be out.

And Maeve wasn't the only one paying attention. Laura was starting to give Georgia contemplative looks that had to mean she was wondering about all the time Georgia and Sean were spending together.

Keeping her voice cool and her manner even cooler, Georgia said only, "Sean's been great. He's helped me get the paperwork going on getting my business license—" Which was turning out to be more complicated than she'd anticipated.

"He's a sharp one, is Sean," Maeve said. "No one better at wangling his way around to what he wants in the end."

"Uh-huh."

"Maggie Culhane told me yesterday that she and Colleen Leary were having tea at the pub and heard Sean talking to Brian Connor about his mum's cottage, it standing empty this last year or more."

Georgia sighed inwardly. The grapevine in Dunley was really incredible.

"Yes, Sean was asking about the cottage for me. I'd really like to live in the village if I can."

"I see," Maeve murmured, her gaze on Georgia as sharp as any cop's, waiting for a confession.

"Oh, look," Georgia blurted, "here comes Mary Donohue with the keys to the store."

Thank God, she thought, grateful for the reprieve in the conversation. Maeve was a sweetie, but she had a laserlike focus that Georgia would just as soon avoid. And she and Sean were keeping whatever it was between them quiet. There was no need for anyone else to know, anyway. Neither one of them was interested in feeding the local gossips—and Georgia really didn't want to hear advice from her sister.

"Sorry I'm late," Mary called out when she got closer. "I was showing a farm to a client, and wouldn't you know he'd be late and then insist on walking over every bloody blade of grass in the fields?"

She shook her mass of thick red hair back from her face, produced a key from her suitcase-sized purse and opened the door to the shop. "Now then," she announced, standing back to allow Georgia to pass in front of her. "If this isn't perfect for what you're wanting, I'll be shocked."

It *was* perfect, Georgia thought, wandering into the empty space. The floor was wood, scarred from generations of feet tracking across its surface. But with some polish, it would look great. The walls were in need of a coat of paint, but all in all, the place really worked for Georgia. In her mind, she set up a desk and chairs and shelves with samples stacked neatly. She walked through, the heels of her boots clacking against the floor. She gave a quick look to the small kitchen in the back, the closet-sized bath and the storeroom. She'd already been through the place once and knew it was the one for her. But today was to settle the last of her nerves before she signed the rental papers.

The main room was long and narrow, and the window let in a wide swath of daylight even in the gray afternoon. She had a great view of the main street, looking out directly across the road at a small bakery where she could go for her lunch every day and get tea and a sandwich. She'd be a part of Dunley, and she could grow the kind of business she'd always wanted to have.

Georgia breathed deep and realized that Mary was giving her spiel, and she grinned when she realized she would never have to do that herself, again. Maeve wandered the room, inspecting the space as if she'd never seen it before. Outside, two or three curious villagers began to gather, peering into the windows, hands cupped around their eyes.

Another quick smile from Georgia as she turned to Mary and said, "Yes. It's perfect."

Sean came rushing through the front door just in time to hear her announcement. He gave her a wide smile and walked across the room to her. Dropping both hands onto her shoulders, he gave her a fast, hard kiss, and said, "That's for congratulations."

Georgia's lips buzzed in reaction to that spontaneous kiss even while she worried about Maeve and Mary being witnesses to it. Sean didn't seem to mind, though. But then, he was such an outgoing guy, maybe no one would think anything of it.

"We used handshakes for that in my day," Maeve murmured.

"Ah, Maeve my darlin', did you want a kiss, too?" Sean swept the older woman up, planted a quick kiss on her mouth and had her back on her feet, swatting the air at him a second later.

"Go on, Sean Connolly, you always were free with your kisses."

"He was indeed," Mary said with a wink for Georgia. "Talk of the village he was. Why when my Kitty was young, I used to warn her about our Sean here."

Sean slapped one hand to his chest in mock offense. "You're a hard woman, Mary Donohue, when you know Kitty was the first to break my heart."

Mary snorted. "Hard to break a thing that's never been used."

No one else seemed to notice, but Georgia saw a flash of something in Sean's eyes that made her wonder if

Mary's words hadn't cut a little deeper than she'd meant. But a moment later, Sean was speaking again in that teasing tone she knew so well.

"Pretty women were meant to be kissed. You can't blame me for doing what's expected, can you?"

"You always did have as much brass as a marching band," Maeve told him, but she was smiling.

"So then, it's settled." Sean looked from Georgia to Mary. "You'll be taking the shop."

"I am," she said, "if Mary's brought the papers with her."

"I have indeed," that woman said and again dipped into her massive handbag.

Georgia followed her off a few steps to take care of business while Sean stood beside Maeve and watched her go.

"And just what kind of deviltry are you up to this time, Sean Connolly?" Maeve whispered.

Sean didn't look at the older woman. Couldn't seem to tear his gaze off of Georgia. Nothing new there. She had been uppermost in his mind for the past two weeks. Since the first time he'd touched her, Sean had thought about little else but touching her again. He hadn't meant to kiss her like that in front of witnesses—especially Maeve—but damned if he'd been able to help himself.

"I don't know what you mean, Maeve."

"Oh, yes," the older woman said with a knowing look, "it's clear I've confused you..."

"Leave off, Maeve," he murmured. "I'm here only to help if I can."

"Being the generous sort," she muttered right back.

He shot her a quick look and sighed. There was no putting anything over on Maeve Carrol. When they were boys, he and Ronan had tried too many times to count to get away with some trouble or other only to be stopped short by the tiny woman now beside him.

Frowning a bit, he turned to watch Georgia as she read over the real estate agent's papers. She was small but, as he knew too well, curvy in all the right places. In her faded blue jeans and dark scarlet, thickly knit sweater, she looked too good. Standing here in this worn, empty store, she looked vivid. Alive. In a way that made everything else around her look as gray as the skies covering Dunley.

"Ronan says you haven't been by the house much," Maeve mentioned.

"Ah, well, I'm giving them time to settle in with Fiona. Don't need people dropping in right and left."

"You've been *dropping* in since you were a boy, Sean." She clucked her tongue and mused, "Makes a body wonder what you've found that's kept you so busy."

"I've got a business to run, don't I?" he argued in a lame defense, for Maeve knew as well as he did that his presence wasn't required daily at the offices of Irish Air. There was plenty of time for him to stop in at Ronan's house as he always had. But before, he hadn't been trying to cover up an affair with his...what was Georgia to him? A cousin-in-law? He shook his head. Didn't matter. "I'll go to the house, Maeve."

"See that you do. Ronan's wanting to show off his baby girl to you, so mind you go to there soon."

"I will and all," he assured her, then snatched at his ringing cell phone as he would a lifeline tossed into a churning sea. Lifting one finger to Maeve as if to tell her one moment, he turned and answered, "Sean Connolly."

A cool, dispassionate voice started speaking and he actually *felt* a ball of ice drop into the pit of his stomach.

"Repeat that if you please," he ordered, though he didn't want to hear the news again. He had to have the information.

His gaze moved to Georgia, who had turned to look at him, a question in her eyes. His tone of voice must have alerted her to a problem.

"I understand," he said into the phone. "I'm on my way."

He snapped the phone closed.

Georgia walked up to him. "What is it?"

Sean could hardly say the words, but he forced them out. "It's my mother. She's in hospital." It didn't sound real. Didn't feel real. But according to the nurse who'd just hung up on him, it was. "She's had a heart attack."

"Ah, Sean," Maeve said, sympathy rich in her voice.

He didn't want pity. More than that though, he didn't want to be in a position to need it. "She's in Westport. I have to go."

He headed for the door, mind already racing two or three steps ahead. He'd get to the hospital, talk to the doctors, then figure out what to do next. His mother was hale and hearty—usually—so he wouldn't worry until he knew more. An instant later, he told himself *Bollocks to that,* as he realized the worry and fear had already started.

Georgia was right behind him. "Let me come with you."

"No." He stopped, looked down into her eyes and saw her concern for him and knew that if she were with him, her fears would only multiply his own. Sounded foolish even to him, but he had to do this alone. "I have to go—"

Then he hit the door at a dead run and kept running until he'd reached his car.

* * *

Ailish Connolly was not the kind of woman to be still.

So seeing his mother lying in a hospital bed, hooked up to machinery that beeped and whistled an ungodly tune was nearly enough to bring Sean to his knees. Disjointed but heartfelt prayers raced through his mind as he reached for the faith of his childhood in this time of panic.

It had been too long since he'd been to Mass. Hadn't graced a church with his presence in too many years to count. But now, at this moment, he wanted to fling himself at the foot of an altar and beg God for help.

Sean shoved one hand through his hair and bit back the impatience clawing inside him. He felt so bloody helpless, and that, he thought, was the worst of it. Nothing he could do but sit and wait, and as he wasn't a patient man by nature…the waiting came hard.

The private room he had arranged for his mother smelled like her garden, since he'd bought every single flower in the gift shop. That was what he'd been reduced to. Shopping for flowers while his mother lay still and quiet. He wasn't accustomed to being unable to affect change around him.

Sean Connolly was a man who got things done. Always. Yet here, in the Westport hospital, he could do not a bloody thing to get action. To even get a damned doctor to answer his questions. So far, all he'd managed to do was irritate the nurses and that, he knew, was no way to gain cooperation. Irish nurses were a tough bunch and took no trouble from anyone.

Sitting beside his mother's bed in a torture chair designed to make visiting an ordeal, Sean braced his elbows on his knees and cupped his face in his palms. It had been only his mother and he for so long, he couldn't remember his life any other way. His father had died when Sean was just a boy, and Ailish had done the heroic task of two parents.

Then when Ronan's parents had died in that accident, Ailish had stepped in for him, as well. She was strong, remarkably self-possessed and until today, Sean would have thought, invulnerable. He lifted his gaze to the small woman with short, dark red hair. There was gray mixed with the red, he noticed for the first time. Not a lot, but enough to shake him.

When had his mother gotten old? Why was she here? She'd been to lunch with her friends and had felt a pain that had worried her enough she had come to the hospital to have it checked. And once the bloody doctors got their hands on you, you were good and fixed, Sean thought grimly, firing a glare at the closed door and the busy corridor beyond.

They'd slapped Ailish in to be examined and now, several hours later, he was still waiting to hear what the dozens of tests they'd done would tell them. The waiting, as he had told Georgia not so very long ago, was the hardest.

Georgia.

He wished he had brought her with him. She was a calm, cool head, and at the moment he needed that. Because what he was tempted to do was have his mother transferred to a bigger hospital in Dublin. To fly in specialists. "To *buy* the damned hospital so *someone* would come in and talk to me."

"Sean," his mother whispered, opening her eyes and turning her face toward him, "don't swear."

"Mother." He stood up, curled one hand around the bar of her bed and reached down with the other to take hers in his. "How are you?"

"I'm fine," she insisted. "Or I was, having a lovely nap until my son's cursing woke me."

"Sorry." She still had the ability to make him feel like a guilty boy. He supposed all mothers had that power, though at the moment, only *his* mother concerned him. "But no one will talk to me. No one will tell me a bloody—" He cut himself off. "I can't get answers from anyone in this place."

"Perhaps they don't have any to give yet," she pointed out.

That didn't ease his mind any.

Her face was pale, her sharp green eyes were a little watery, and the pale wash of freckles on her cheeks stood out like gold paint flicked atop a saucer of milk.

His heart actually ached to see her here. Like this. Fear wasn't something he normally even considered, but the thought of his mother perhaps being at death's bleeding door with not a doctor in sight cut him right down to the bone.

"Do you know what I was thinking," she said softly, giving her son's hand a gentle squeeze, "when they were sticking their wires and such to me?"

He could imagine. She must have been terrified. "No," he said. "Tell me."

"All I could think was, I was going to die and leave you alone," she murmured, and a single tear fell from the corner of her eye to roll down her temple and into her hair.

"There'll be no talk of dying," he told her, instinctively fighting against the fear that crouched inside him. "And I'm not alone. I've friends, and Ronan and Laura, and now the baby…"

"And no family of your own," she pointed out.

"And what're you then?" Sean teased.

She shook her head and fixed her gaze with his. "You

should have a wife. A family, Sean. A man shouldn't live his life alone."

It was an old argument. Ailish was forever trying to marry off her only child. But now, for the first time, Sean felt guilty. She should have been concerned for herself; instead she was worried for him. Worried *about* him. He hated that she was lying there so still and pale, and that there was nothing he could do for her. Bloody hell, he couldn't even get the damn doctor to step into the room.

"Ronan's settled and happy now," Ailish said softly. "And so should you be."

Her fingers felt small and fragile in his grip, and the fear and worry bottled up inside Sean seemed to spill over. "I am," he blurted before he was even aware of speaking.

Her gaze sharpened. "You are what?"

"Settled," he lied valiantly. He hadn't planned to. But seeing her worry needlessly had torn something inside Sean and had him telling himself that this at least, he could do for her. A small lie couldn't be that bad, could it, if it brought peace? And what if she *was* dying, God forbid, but how was he to know since no one would tell him anything. Wouldn't it be better for her to go believing that Sean was happy?

"I'm engaged," he continued, and gave his mother a smile. "I was going to tell you next week," he added, as the lie built up steam and began to travel on its own.

Her eyes shone and a smile curved her mouth even as twin spots of color flushed her pale cheeks. "That's wonderful," she said. "Who is she?"

Who indeed?

Brain racing, Sean could think of only one woman who would fit this particular bill, but even he couldn't drag Georgia into this lie without some warning. "I'll tell you as soon as you're fit and out of here."

Now those sharp green eyes narrowed on him. "If this is a trick…"

He slapped one hand to his chest and hoped not to be struck down as he said, "Would I lie about something this important?"

"No," she said after a long moment, "no, you wouldn't."

Guilt took another nibble of his soul.

"There you are then," he pronounced. "Now try to get some sleep."

She nodded, closed her eyes and still with a smile on her face, was asleep in minutes. Which left Sean alone with his thoughts—

A few hours later the doctor finally deigned to make an appearance, and though Sean was furious, he bit his tongue and was glad he had. A minor heart attack. No damage to her heart, really, just a warning of sorts for Ailish to slow down a bit and take better care of herself.

The doctor also wanted a few more tests to be sure of his results, which left Sean both relieved and worried. A minor heart attack was still serious enough. Was she well enough to find out he'd…*exaggerated* his engagement?

She would be in hospital for a week, resting under doctor's orders, so Sean wouldn't have to decide about telling her the truth right away. But he *did* have to have a chat with Georgia. Just in case.

Four

He left his mother sleeping and made his way out of the hospital, grateful to leave behind its smell of antiseptic and fear. Stepping into a soft, evening mist, Sean stopped dead when a familiar voice spoke up.

"Sean?"

He turned and felt a well of pleasure open up inside as Georgia walked toward him. "What're you doing here?" he asked, wrapping both arms around her and holding on.

She hugged him, then pulled her head back to look up at him. "When we didn't hear anything, I got worried. So I came here to wait for you. How's your mom?"

Pleasure tangled with gratitude as he realized just how much he'd needed to see her. He'd been a man alone for most of his adult life, never asking for anything, never expecting anyone to go an extra meter for him. Yet here she was, stepping out of the mist and cold, and Sean had never been happier to see anyone.

"She's well, though the doctor's holding on to her for a week or so. More tests, he says, and he wants her to rest. Never could get my mother to slow down long enough to *rest,* so God help the nurses trying to hold her down in that bed," he said, dropping a quick kiss on her forehead. "Scared me, Georgia. I don't even remember the last time anything has."

"Family does that to you," she told him. "But she's okay?"

"Will be," he said firmly. "It was a 'minor' heart attack, they say. No permanent damage, though, so that's good. She's to take it easy for a few weeks, no upsets. But yes, she'll be fine."

"Good news." Georgia's gaze narrowed on him. "So why do you look more worried than relieved?"

"I'll tell you all. But first, I've a need to get away from this place. Feels like I've been here for years instead of hours." Frowning, he looked out at the car park. "How did you get here?"

"Called a cab." She shrugged. "Laura was going to drive me, but I told her and Ronan that I'd be fine and you'd bring me home."

"As I will," he said, taking her arm and steering her toward his car. "But first, we'll go to my house. We need to talk."

"You'll tell me on the way?"

"I think not," he hedged. "I'm a man in desperate need of a beer, and I'm thinking you'll be needing wine to hear this."

There wasn't enough wine in the world.

"Are you insane?" Georgia jumped off the comfortable sofa in Sean's front room and stared down at him in stunned shock. "I mean, seriously. Maybe we should have had *you* examined at the hospital while we were there."

Sean huffed out a breath and took a long drink of the beer he'd poured for himself as soon as they reached his home. Watching him, Georgia took a sip of her Chardonnay, to ease the tightness in her own throat.

Then he leaned forward and set the glass of beer onto the table in front of him. "I'm not insane, no. Crazy perhaps, but not insane."

"Fine line, if you ask me."

He pushed one hand through his hair and muttered, "I'm not explaining this well a'tall."

"Oh, I don't know." Georgia sipped at her wine, then set her own glass down beside his. Still standing, she crossed both arms over her chest and said, "You were pretty clear. You want me to *pretend* to be engaged to you so you can lie to your mother. That about cover it?"

He scowled and stood up, Georgia thought, just so he could loom over her from his much greater height.

"Well, when you put it like that," he muttered, "it sounds—"

"Terrible? Is that the word you're looking for?"

He winced as he scrubbed one hand across his face. Georgia felt a pang of sympathy for him even though a part of her wanted to kick him.

"I thought she was dying."

"So you lied to her to give her a good send-off?"

He glared at her, and for the first time since she'd known him, she wasn't seeing the teasing, laughing, charming Sean...but instead the hard-lined owner of Irish Air. This was the man who'd bought out a struggling airline and built it into the premier luxury line in the world. The man who had become a billionaire through sheer strength of will. His eyes flashed with heat, with temper, and his mouth, the one she knew so well, was now flattened into a grim line.

Georgia, who had a temper of her own and just as hard a head, was unimpressed.

"If you think I enjoy lying to her, you're wrong."

"Well, good, because I *like* your mother."

"As do I," he argued.

"Then tell her the truth."

"I will," he countered, "as soon as the doctor says she's well again. Until then, would it really be so bad to let her believe a small lie?"

"Small." She shook her head and walked toward the wide stone hearth, where a fire burned against the cold night. On the mantel above the fire were framed family photos. Sean and Ronan. Sean and his mother. Laura and Georgia captured forever the day Ronan and Sean had taken them to the Burren—a lonely, desolate spot just a few miles outside Galway. Family was important to him, she knew that. Seeing these photos only brought that truth back to her.

She turned her back to the flames and looked at him, across the room from her. Sean's and Ronan's houses were both huge, sprawling manors, but Sean's was more…casual, she supposed was the right word. He'd lived alone here, but for his housekeeper and any number of people who worked on the estate, so he'd done as he pleased with the furniture.

Oversize sofas covered in soft fabric in muted shades of gray and blue crowded the room. Heavy, carved wooden tables dotted the interior, brass-based reading lamps tossed golden circles of light across gleaming wood floors and midnight-blue rugs. The walls were stone as well, interspersed with heavy wooden beams, and the wide front windows provided a view of a lawn that looked as if the gardener had gone over it on his knees with a pair of scissors, it was so elegantly tended.

"Is it really such a chore to pretend to be mad about me?" he asked, a half smile curving his mouth.

She looked at him and thought, no, pretending to be crazy about him wasn't a problem. Which should probably *be* a problem, she told herself, but that was a worry for another day.

"You want me to lie to Ailish."

"For only a while," he said smoothly. "To give me time to see her settled." He frowned a bit and added quietly, "She's...important to me, Georgia. I don't want her hurt."

God, was there anything sexier than a man unafraid to show his love for someone? Knowing how much Ailish meant to Sean touched Georgia deeply, but she was still unconvinced that his plan was a good one. Still, she remembered clearly how devastated she had been when she'd discovered all of her ex-husband's lies to her. Wouldn't Ailish feel the same sort of betrayal?

She shook her head slowly. "And you don't think she'll be hurt when she discovers she's been tricked?"

"Ah, but she won't find that out, will she?" Sean said, and he was smiling again, his temper having blown away as fast as it had come. "When the time is right, you'll throw me over, as well you should, and I'll bravely go on with my heart shattered to jagged pieces."

She snorted a laugh before she could stop it.

"So I get to be the bad guy, too?" She walked back, picked up her wine and took another sip. "Wow, I'm a lucky woman, all right. You remember I'm moving to Dunley, don't you? I'll see Ailish all the time, Sean, and she's going to think I'm a hideous person for dumping her son."

"She won't blame you," he assured her, "I'll see to it."

"Uh-huh."

"Georgia love," he said with a sigh, "you're my only chance at pulling this off."

"I don't like it."

"Of course you don't, being an honest woman." He plucked the wineglass from her fingers and set it aside. Then, stroking his hands up and down her arms, he added, "But being a warm-hearted, generous one as well, you can see this is the best way, can't you?"

"You think you can smooth me into this with a caress and a kiss?"

He bent down until his eyes were fixed on hers. "Aye, I do." Before she could respond to that arrogant admission, he added, "But I don't think I'll have to, will I? You've a kind heart, Georgia, and I know you can see why I've to do this."

Okay, yes, she could. Irritating to admit that even to herself. She understood the fear that must have choked him when he thought his mother was going to die. But damn it. Memories fluttered in her mind like a swarm of butterflies. "Lies never go well, Sean."

"But we're not lying to each other now, are we? So between the two of us, everything is on the up and up, and my mother will get over the disappointment—when she's well."

"It's not *just* your mother, though," she said. "The whole village will know. They'll all think I'm a jerk for dumping you."

"Hah!" Sean grinned widely. "Most of those in Dunley will think you a fool for agreeing to marry me in the first place and will swear you've come to your senses when we end it. And if that doesn't do the job, I'll take the blame entirely."

She laughed, because he looked so pleased with that statement. "You're completely shameless, aren't you?"

"Absolutely," he agreed, with that grin that always managed to make her stomach take a slow bump and roll. "So will you do it then, Georgia? Will you pretend to be engaged to me?"

She was tempted, she could admit that much to herself. It was a small thing, after all. Just to help her lover out of a tight spot. And oh, he was a wonderful lover, she thought, her heart beginning to trip wildly in her chest. The time spent with him in the past couple of weeks had been…fabulous. But this was something else again.

"I can help you get your business license," he offered. "You're bogged down in the mire of bureaucratic speak, and I don't know as you'd noticed or not, but things in Ireland move at their own pace. You could be a woman with a walker by the time you got that license pushed through on your own."

She gave him a hard look. "But you're a magician?"

"I've a way about me, that's true. But also, I know some of those that are in charge of these things and frankly, as the owner of Irish Air, I carry a bit more weight to my words than you would."

He could. Darn it. She'd already seen for herself that working her way through the reams of paperwork was going to be mind-boggling.

"I could see you settled and ready for business much faster than you could do it on your own."

"Are you trying to bribe me?"

He grinned, unashamed. "I am and doing a damn fine job of it if you ask me."

Staring up into his brown eyes, shining now with the excitement for his plan, Georgia knew she was pretty much done. And let's face it, she told herself, he'd had her from the jump. Not only was it a great excuse to keep their affair going—but she knew how worried he was about Ailish and she felt for him. He had probably never doubted for a moment that he'd be able to talk her into joining him in his insanity. Even *before* the really superior bribe.

He was unlike anyone she'd ever known, Georgia thought. Everything about him was outrageous. Why wouldn't a proposal from Sean Connolly be the same?

"And, did you know there's a cottage for sale at the edge of the village?"

"Is that the one I hear you were talking to someone named Brian about?"

"Ah, the Dunley express," he said with a grin. "Talk about it in the pub and it's as good as published in the paper. No, this isn't Brian's mum's place. He's rented it just last week to Sinead and Michael when they come home."

"Oh." Well, there went a perfectly good cottage. "I spoke to Mary this afternoon, and she didn't say a thing about a cottage for sale."

"She doesn't know all," Sean said, bending to plant one quick, hard kiss on her lips. "For example, I own two of the cottages near the close at the end of main. Not far from your new shop..."

That last bit he let hang there long enough for Georgia to consider it. Then he continued.

"They're small, but well kept. Close to the village center and with a faery wood in the back."

She shook her head and laughed. "A what?"

He smiled, that delicious, slow curve of his mouth that promised wickedness done to perfection. "A faery wood, where if you stand and make a wish on the full of the moon, you might get just what your heart yearns for." He paused. "Or, the faeries might snatch you away to live forever in their raft beneath the trees."

With the song of Ireland in his voice, even the crazy sounded perfectly reasonable. "Faeries."

"You'd live in Ireland and dismiss them?" he challenged, his eyes practically twinkling now with good humor and banked laughter.

"Sean…"

"I could be convinced to make you a very good deal on either of the cottages, if…"

"You're evil," she said softly. "My mother used to warn me about men like you."

"An intelligent woman to be sure. I liked her very much when we met at Ronan's wedding."

Her mother had liked him, too. But then, her mom liked everybody. Georgia could remember being like that once upon a time. Before her ex-husband had left her for her cheerleader cousin and cleaned out their joint accounts on his way out of town. Just remembering the betrayal, the hurt, stiffened her spine even while her mind raced. Too many thoughts piling together were jumbled up in possibilities and possible disasters.

She was torn, seriously. She really did like Sean's mother and she hated the thought of lying to her. But Sean would be the *real* liar, right? Oh, man, even she couldn't buy that one. She would be in this right up to her neck if she said yes. But how could she not? Sean was offering to help her get her new life started, and all she had to do was pretend to be in love with him.

And that wasn't going to be too difficult, she warned herself. Just standing here beside him was dangerous. She knew all too well what it was like to have his hands and mouth on her. Having a lover like Sean—much less a fiancé, pretend or not—was really a slippery slope toward something she had to guard against.

She wasn't interested in trusting another man. Giving her heart over to him. Giving him the chance to crush her again. Sure, Sean was nothing like her ex, but he was still *male*.

"What do you say, Georgia?" he asked, reaching down to take her hands in his and give them a squeeze. "Will you pretend-marry me?"

She couldn't think. Not with him holding on to her. Not with his eyes staring into hers. Not with the heat of him reaching for her, promising even *more* heat if she let him get any closer. And if she did that, she would agree to anything, because she well knew the man could have her half out of her mind in seconds.

Georgia pulled her hands free of his and took one long step back. "This isn't the kind of thing I can decide on in a minute, Sean. There's a lot to consider. So I'll think about it and let you know tomorrow, okay?"

He opened his mouth as if to argue, then, a moment later, changed his mind. Nodding, he closed the distance between them again and pulled her into the circle of his arms. Georgia leaned into him, giving herself this moment to feel the rush of something spectacular that happened every time he touched her.

Kissing the top of her head, he whispered, "Fine then. That'll do. For now."

With him holding on to her, the beat of his heart beneath her ear, Georgia was tempted to do all sorts of things, so she looked away from him, out the window to the rain-drenched evening. Lamps lining the drive shone like diamonds in the gray. But the darkness and the incessant rain couldn't disguise the beauty that was Ireland.

Just like, she thought, looking up at Sean, a lie couldn't

hide what was already between the two of them. She didn't know where it was going, but she had a feeling the ride was going to be much bumpier than she had planned.

"I feel like I haven't slept in years," Laura groaned over her coffee the following morning.

"At least you can have caffeine again," Georgia said.

"Yes." Her sister paused. "Is it wrong to be nearly grateful that Fiona had no interest in nursing just so I can have coffee again?"

"If it is, I won't tell."

"You're the best." Laura slouched in a chair near the end of the couch where Georgia sat, checking email on her computer tablet.

Though she'd never been much of a morning person, it was hard to remain crabby when you got to sit in this beautiful parlor sipping coffee every morning. Of course, the baby had jumbled life in the manor, but she had to admit she loved being around her niece. Georgia glanced out the window at a sun-washed vista of sloping yard and trees beginning to lose their leaves for winter. For the first time in days, the sky was clear, but the cold Irish wind was tossing leaves into the air and making the trees dance and sway.

"I'm so excited that you're moving to Ireland," Laura said. "I really miss you when you're not around."

Georgia smiled at her sister. "I know, me, too. And it is exciting to move," she said, as she reached out for the silver pot on the rolling tea table in front of them. Hefting it, she refilled both her own and Laura's cups. Tea might be the big thing over here, but thankfully Patsy Brennan was willing to brew a pot of coffee for the Page sisters every morning. "Also, moving is terrifying. Not only going to a new place and starting over, but it's all the logistics of the thing. Canceling mail and utilities, starting them up somewhere else, and the packing."

Georgia shuddered and took a sip of coffee to bolster her.

"I get that. I was worried when I first moved here with Ronan, but everything went great."

"You had Ronan."

"And you have *me*."

"Ever the optimist," Georgia noted.

"No point in being a pessimist," Laura countered. "If you go around all grim, expecting the worst, when it happens, you've been suffering longer than you had to."

Georgia just blinked at her. "I'll work on that one and let you know when I figure it out."

Laura grinned, then sobered up again. "I wish you'd reconsider living here with us. There's plenty of room."

She knew her sister meant it, and having her offer was really wonderful. Even though having a secret affair was hard to manage when you were living with your sister. "I know, and I appreciate the offer. Just like I appreciate you letting me stay here when I visit. But I want my own place, Laura."

"Yeah, I know."

Morning light filtered into the room, and the winter sunshine was pale and soft. The baby monitor receiver that Laura carried with her at all times sat on the coffee table in front of them, and from it came the soft sounds of Fiona's breathing and the tiny sniffling sounds she made as she slept.

"Yesterday, Sean told me he owns a couple of cottages at the edge of the village," Georgia said. "He's going to sell me one of them."

"And that," Laura said thoughtfully, "brings us to the

main question for the day. What's going on with you and Sean?"

She went still and dropped her gaze to the black coffee in her cup. "Nothing."

"Right. What am I, blind? I gave birth in the hospital, Georgia," her sister pointed out, "I didn't have a lobotomy."

"Laura…" Georgia had known this was coming. Actually, it was probably only because Laura was so wrapped up in Fiona that she hadn't noticed earlier. Laura wasn't stupid and as she just mentioned, not blind, either.

"I can see how you guys are around each other," Laura was saying, tapping her fingernails lightly against the arm of the chair. "He watches you."

"Oooh, that's suspicious."

"I said he *watches* you. Like a man dying of thirst and you're a fountain of ice-cold water."

Something inside her stirred and heat began to crawl through Georgia's veins, in spite of her effort to put a stop to it. After that proposal Sean had made last night, he'd kissed her senseless, then dropped her off here at the manor, leaving Georgia so stirred up she'd hardly slept. Now, just the thought of Sean was enough to light up the ever-present kindling inside her.

Shaking her head, she said only, "Leave it alone, Laura."

"Sure. I'll do that. I'm sorry. Have we met?" Laura leaned toward her. "Honey, don't get me wrong. I'm glad you're having fun finally. God knows it took you long enough to put what's-his-name in the past—"

At the mention of Georgia's ex, she frowned. Okay, fine. It had taken her some time to get past the fury of being used, betrayed and then finally, publicly *dumped*.

But she figured most women would have come out of that situation filled with righteous fury.

"Gee, thanks."

"—I just don't want you to get crushed again."

"What happened to that optimism?"

Laura frowned at her. "This is different. What if you guys crash and burn? Then you'll be living here, with Sean right around the corner practically and seeing him all the time and you'll be miserable. I don't want that for you."

Georgia sighed and gave her sister's hand a pat. "I know. But you don't get to decide that, Laura. And we're not going to crash and burn. We're just…"

"…yeah?"

"I was going to say we're just lovers."

"There's no 'just' about it for you, Georgia," Laura sputtered. "Not for either one of us. We're not built that way. We don't do 'easy.'"

"I know that, too," Georgia argued, "but I did the cautious thing for years, and what did it get me? I thought Mike was the one, remember? Did everything right. Dated for two years, was engaged for one of those two. Big wedding, nice house, working together to build something, and what happened?"

Laura winced.

Georgia saw it and nodded. "Exactly. Mike runs off with Misty, who, if she had two thoughts running around in that tiny brain of hers, would rattle like BBs in a jar."

Laura smiled, but sadly. "That's no reason to jump into something with a man like Sean."

Suddenly forced to defend the man she was currently sleeping with, Georgia said, "What does that mean, 'a man like Sean'? He's charming and treats me great. We have fun together, and that's all either one of us is looking for."

"For now."

Georgia shook her head and smiled. "All I'm interested in at the moment is 'for now,' Laura. I did the whole cautious thing for way too long. Maybe it's time to cut loose a little. Stop thinking nonstop about the future and just enjoy today."

A long moment passed before Laura sighed and said, "Maybe you're right. Sean is a sweetie, but Georgia—"

"Don't worry," she said, holding up one hand to stave off any more advice. "I'm not looking for marriage and family. I don't know that I ever will."

"Of course you will," Laura told her, sympathy and understanding shining in her eyes. "That's who you are. But if this is what you need right now, I'm on your side."

"Thanks. And," Georgia added, "as long as we're talking about this, you should know that last night Sean asked me to help him out."

In a few short sentences, she explained Sean's plan and watched Laura's mouth drop open. "You can't be serious."

"I think I am."

"Let me count the ways this could go bad."

"Do me a favor and don't, okay?" Georgia glanced down at her email and idly deleted a couple of the latest letters from people offering to send her the winnings to contests she'd never entered. "I've thought about it, and I understand why he's doing it."

"So do I. That doesn't make it a good idea."

"What's not a good idea?" Ronan asked, as he walked into the room and paused long enough to kiss his wife good morning before reaching out to grab a cup and pour himself some coffee.

"Your idiot cousin," Laura started, firing a glare at her

husband as if this were all his fault, "wants my sister to pretend they're engaged."

While Laura filled Ronan in, Georgia sat back and concentrated on her coffee. She had a feeling she was going to need all the caffeine she could get.

Five

When Laura finally wound down and sat in her chair, alternately glowering at Ronan and then her sister, Georgia finally spoke up.

"Sean can sell me a cottage," she said calmly. "He can help push through my business license and speed things up along the bureaucratic conga line."

"Ronan can do that, too, you know."

"I know he can," Georgia said with a smile for her brother-in-law. "Sean's already volunteered."

"And…" Laura said.

"And what?"

"And you're already lovers, so this is going to complicate things."

"Oh," Ronan muttered, "when did that happen? No. Never mind. I don't need to know this."

"It's not going to get complicated," Georgia insisted.

"Everything gets complicated," Laura argued. "Heck,

look at me! I broke up with Ronan last year, remember? Now here I sit, in Ireland, married, with a baby daughter."

Ronan asked wryly, "Are you complaining?"

Laura shot a look at the man studying her through warm brown eyes. "No way. Wouldn't change a thing. I'm just saying," she continued, shifting her gaze back to Georgia, "that even when you think you know what's going to happen, things suddenly turn upside down on you."

A warbling cry erupted from the baby monitor on the table in front of Laura. Picking it up, she turned off the volume and stood.

"I have to go get the baby, but we're not done here," she warned, as she left the dining room.

"Laura's just worried for you." Ronan poured himself more coffee, then sat back and crossed his legs, propping one foot on the opposite knee.

"I know." She looked at him and asked, "But you've known Sean forever. What do you think?"

"I think I warned Sean to keep his distance from you already, for all the good that's done." Then he thought about it for a moment or two, and said, "It's a good idea."

Georgia smiled and eased back in her chair. "Glad to hear you say that."

"But," he added.

"There's always a *but,* isn't there?"

"Right enough," he said. "I can see why Sean wants to do this. Keep his mother happy until she's well. And you helping him is a grand thing as long as you remember that Sean's not the man to *actually* fall for."

"I'm not an idiot," Georgia reminded him.

"And who knows that better than I?" Ronan countered with a smile. "You helped me out last year when Laura was making my life a misery—"

"You're welcome."

"—and I'll do the same now. Sean is a brother to me, and so if he hurts you and I'm forced to kill him, it would pain me."

Georgia grinned. "Thanks. I never had a big brother threaten to beat up a boy who was mean to me."

He toasted her with his coffee cup. "Well, you do now."

She laughed a little. "Good to know."

"You'd already made up your mind to go along with Sean's plan, even before you told Laura, hadn't you?"

"Just about," she admitted. But until Ronan had thrown in on her side, she had still had a few doubts. Being close with Sean was no hardship, but getting much closer could be dangerous to her own peace of mind. Laura was right. Georgia wasn't the "take a lover, use him and lose him" kind of woman. So her heart would be at risk unless she guarded it vigilantly.

"So you've signed your rental agreement on the shop?"

"I did, and I'm going into Galway this morning to look at furnishings." She glanced down at her computer tablet as a sound signaled an incoming email. "I'm really excited about the store, too. Of course it needs some fresh paint and—" She broke off as her gaze skimmed the e-vite she had just received. "You have *got* to be kidding me."

"What is it?" All serious now, Ronan demanded, "What's wrong?"

Georgia hardly heard him over the roaring in her ears. She read the email again and then once more, just to be sure she was seeing it right. She was.

"That miserable, rotten, cheating, lying…"

"Who's that then?"

"My *ex*-husband and my *ex*-cousin," Georgia grumbled. "Of all the— I can't believe this. I mean seriously, could this be any more tacky? Even for *them?*"

"Ah," Ronan muttered. "This may be more in Laura's line…"

Georgia tossed her computer tablet to the couch cushion beside her, set her coffee cup down with a clatter and stood up, riding the wings of pure rage. "I'll see you later, Ronan."

"What?" He stood too and watched as she headed for the back door that led to the stone patio, the garden and the fields beyond. "Where are you going? What am I to tell Laura?"

"Tell her I just got engaged."

Then she was through the door and across the patio.

She could have taken a car and driven along the narrow, curving road to Sean's place. But as angry as she was, Georgia couldn't have sat still for that long. Instead, she took the shortcut. Straight across a sunlit pasture so green it hurt her eyes to look at it. Stone fences rambled across the fields, and she was forced to scramble over them to go on her way.

Normally, she loved this walk. On the right was the round tower that stood near an ancient cemetery on Ronan's land. To her left was Lough Mask, a wide lake fringed by more trees swaying in the wind. In the distance, she heard the whisper of the ocean and the low grumbling of a farmer's tractor. The sky above was a brilliant blue, and the wind that flew at her carried the chill of the sea.

Georgia was too furious to feel the cold.

Her steps were quick, and she kept her gaze focused on her target. The roof of Sean's manor house was just visible above the tips of the trees, and she headed there with a steely determination.

She crossed the field, walked into the wood and only then remembered Sean saying something about the faeries and how they might snatch her away.

"Well, I'd like to see them try it today," she murmured.

Georgia came out of the thick stand of trees at the edge of Sean's driveway. A wide gravel drive swung in a graceful arch in front of the stone-and-timber manor. Leaded windows glinted in the sunlight. As she neared the house, Sean stepped out and walked to meet her. He was wearing black slacks, a cream-colored sweater and a black jacket. His dark hair ruffled in the wind, and his hands were tucked into his pockets.

"Georgia!" He grinned at her. "I was going to stop to see you on my way to hospital to check in on my mother."

She pushed her tangled hair back from her face and stomped the dew and grass from her knee-high black boots. She wore her favorite, dark green sweater dress, and the wind flipped the hem around her knees. She had one short flash that for something this big, she should have worn something better than a dress she'd had for five years. But then, she wasn't really getting engaged, was she? It was a joke. A pretense.

Just like her first marriage had been.

"Are you all right?" he asked, his smile fading as he really looked at her. Walking closer, he pulled his hands from his pockets and reached out to take hold of her shoulders.

"Really not." Georgia took a deep breath of the cold Irish air and *willed* it to settle some of the roaring heat she still felt inside. It didn't work.

"What's wrong then?"

There was real concern on his face and for that, she

was grateful. Sean was exactly who he claimed to be. There was no hidden agenda with him. There were no secrets. He wouldn't cheat on a woman and sneak out of town with every cent she owned. It wouldn't even occur to him. She could admire that about him since she had already survived the man who was the exact opposite of Sean Connolly.

That thought brought her right back to the reason for her mad rush across the open field.

"You offered me a deal yesterday," she said.

"I did."

"Now I've got one for you."

Sean released her, but didn't step back. His gaze was still fixed on her and concern was still etched on his face. "All right then, let's hear it."

"I don't even know where to start," she said suddenly, then blurted out, "I just got an email from my cousin Misty. The woman my ex-husband ran off with."

"Ah." He nodded as if he could understand now why she was so upset.

"Actually, the email was an e-vite to their *wedding*."

His jaw dropped, and she could have kissed him for that alone. That he would *get* it, right away, no explanation necessary, meant more to Georgia than she could have said.

"She sent you an e-vite?" He snorted a laugh, then noted her scowl and sobered up fast. "Bloody rude."

"You think?" Shaking her head, Georgia started pacing back and forth on the gravel drive, hearing the grinding noise of the pebbles beneath her boots. "First, that she's tacky enough to use e-vites as wedding invitations!" She shot him a look and threw both hands in the air. "Who does that?"

"I wouldn't know."

"Of course you wouldn't, because *no one* does that!" Back to pacing, the *crunch, crunch* of the gravel sounding out in a rapid rhythm. "And really? You send one of your stupid, tacky e-vites to the woman your fiancé cheated on? The one he left for *you?*"

"The pronouns are starting to get confusing, in case you were wondering," Sean told her.

She ignored that. "And Mike. What the hell was *he* thinking?" Georgia demanded. "He thinks it's okay to invite me to his wedding? What're we now? Old *friends?* I'm supposed to be civilized?"

"What fun is civilized?" Sean asked.

"Exactly!" She stabbed a finger at him. "Not that I care who the creep marries and if you ask me, the two of them deserve each other, but why does either one of them think I want to be there to watch the beginning of a marriage that is absolutely doomed from the start?"

"Couldn't say," Sean said.

"No one could, because it doesn't make sense," Georgia continued, letting the words rush from her on a torrent of indignation. Then something occurred to her. "They probably don't expect me to actually *go* to the wedding."

"No?"

"No." She stopped dead, faced Sean and said, "Misty just wants me to *know* that she finally got Mike to marry her. Thinks it'll hurt me somehow."

"And of course she's wrong about that," Sean mused.

She narrowed her eyes on him. "Do I look hurt to you?"

"Not a bit," he said quickly. "You look furious and well you should be."

"Damn right." She set both hands on her hips and tapped the toe of one boot against the gravel, only absently noting the rapid *tappity, tappity, tap* sound. "But you know what? I'm *going* to that wedding. I'm going to be the chill kiss of death for those two at the happy festivities."

Sean laughed. "I do admire a woman with fire in her eyes."

"Then stick around," she snapped. "I'm going to show them just how little they mean to me."

"Good on you," Sean said.

"And the kicker is, I'm going to be arriving at their wedding in Brookhollow, Ohio, with my gorgeous, fabulously wealthy Irish fiancé."

One corner of his mouth tipped up. "Are you now?"

"That's the deal," Georgia said calmly, now that the last of her outrage had been allowed to spill free. "I'll help you keep your mom happy until she's well if you go to this wedding with me and convince everyone there that you're nuts about me."

"That's a deal," he said quickly and walked toward her.

She skipped back a step and held up one hand to keep him at bay. "And you'll help me get my license and sell me that cottage, too, right?"

"Absolutely."

"Okay, then." She huffed out a breath as if she'd been running a marathon.

"We've a deal, Georgia Page, and I think we'll both come out of this for the better."

"I hope you're right," she said and held out her right hand to take his in a handshake.

He smirked and shook his head. "That's no way to seal a deal between lovers."

Then he swooped in, grabbed her tightly and swung her into a dip that had her head spinning even *before* he kissed her blind.

* * *

The next few days flew past.

Georgia could even forget, occasionally, that what was between she and Sean wasn't actually *real*. He played his part so well. The doting fiancé. The man in love. Seriously, if she hadn't known it was an act, she would have tumbled headfirst into love with him.

And wouldn't that be awkward?

True to his word, Sean had pushed through the paperwork for her business license, and in just a week or two she would have it in hand. He sold her one of the cottages he owned and made her such a good deal on it she almost felt guilty, then she reminded herself that it was all part of the agreement they had struck. And with that reminder came the annoying tug of memory about her ex and the wedding Sean would be attending with her.

Georgia squared her shoulders and steeled her spine. She'd made her decision and wouldn't back away now. Besides, her new life was coming together. She had her lover. A shop. A new home.

And all of it built on a tower of lies, her mind whispered.

"The question is," she asked herself aloud, "what part of it will survive when the tower collapses?" Frowning at the pessimistic thoughts that she was determined to avoid, she added, "Not helping."

She had chosen her road and wouldn't change directions now. Whatever happened, she and Sean would deal with it. They were two adults after all. They could have sex. Have…whatever it was they had, without destroying each other. And then, there was the fact that even if she had been willing to consider ending their deal, she was in too deep to find a way out anyway. So instead, she would suck it up, follow the plan Sean had laid out and hope for the best.

Meanwhile, she had a shop to get ready and a new cottage to decorate and furnish.

She stepped back to take a look at her handiwork and smiled at the wash of palest yellow paint on one of the walls of her new office. It was cheerful and just bright enough to ease back the gray days that seemed to be a perpetual part of the Irish life. The smell of paint was strong, so she had propped open the front door. That cold wind she was so accustomed to now whipped through the opening and tugged at her hair as she worked.

All morning, people in the village had been stopping in, to offer help—which Georgia didn't need, since she wanted to do this part herself—or to offer congratulations on her upcoming marriage. So she hardly jumped when a voice spoke up from the doorway.

"It's lovely."

Georgia turned to smile at Ailish as Sean's mother walked into the shop just a step or two ahead of her son.

"Thanks." Georgia smiled at both of them. "I didn't know you were stopping by. Ailish, it's so good to see you out of the hospital."

"It's even better from my perspective," she answered quickly, a soft smile curving her mouth. "I can't tell you how badly I wanted to be home again. Of course, I was planning on going back to my own home in Dublin, but my son insists I stay at the family manor until I'm recovered—which I am even now, thanks very much."

"You're not recovered yet and you'll take it easy as the doctor advised," Sean told her.

"Take it easy," Ailish sniffed. "How'm I to do that with you and everyone else hovering?"

Georgia grinned at the expression of helpless frustration on Sean's face. She understood how he was feeling, but she really identified with Ailish. Georgia didn't appreciate hovering, either. "How're you feeling?"

The smaller woman hurried across the tarp-draped floor and took Georgia in a hard, brief hug. "I'm wonderful is what I am," she said. "Sean's told me your news and I couldn't be happier."

Guilt flew like an arrow and stabbed straight into Georgia's heart. She looked into Ailish's sharp green eyes and felt *terrible* for her part in this lie. But at the same time, she could see that Sean's mother's face was pale and there were shadows beneath those lovely eyes of hers. So she wasn't as well as she claimed and maybe, Georgia thought wildly, that was enough of a reason to carry on with the lie.

"Isn't it lovely that you and your sister both will be here, married and building families?" Ailish sighed at the romance of it. "I couldn't ask for a more perfect daughter-in-law."

"Thank you, Ailish," Georgia said and simply embraced the guilt, accepting that it would now be a part of her life. At least for a while.

"Now," Ailish said, grabbing Georgia's left hand. "Let me see the ring…"

There was no ring.

Georgia curled her fingers into her palm and threw a fast look at Sean who mimed slapping his hand to his forehead.

"We've not picked one out yet," he said quickly. "It has to be just right, doesn't it?"

"Hmm…" Ailish patted Georgia's hand even as she slid a curious look at her son. "Well, I'll look forward to seeing it."

"So," Georgia said into the quiet, "you're not heading home to Dublin?"

"Not for a bit yet," she said, "though I do long for my own things about me."

"The manor was your home until four years ago, mother," Sean reminded her. "There's plenty of your things there, as well. And someone to look after you."

"I don't need a keeper," Ailish told him. "Though there were plenty of times I was convinced you did. Until you had the sense to become engaged to Georgia."

"Thanks very much," Sean muttered, stuffing his hands into the pockets of his slacks.

"Now, if you don't mind, I think I'll go sit in the car again until you're ready to leave, Sean. Georgia," she added, leaning in to kiss her cheek, "I couldn't be happier for the both of you. It'll be a lovely wedding, and you know I think this one should be held in Dunley, as Ronan and Laura were married in California."

"Um, sure," Georgia said, as the pile of lies she was standing on grew higher and higher. "Only fair."

"Exactly." Ailish took a breath and let it slide from her lungs as she smiled. "Have you thought about when the wedding will be?"

"We really haven't gotten that far yet," Sean told her. "What with Georgia opening a new business and moving here and all, we've been too busy to set a date."

"Sometime soon then," Ailish went on in a rush. "Perhaps a Christmas wedding? Wouldn't that be lovely? Sean will send a plane for your parents of course, and perhaps they'd like to come out early, so we could all work on the wedding preparations together."

"I'll, um, ask them."

"Wonderful." Ailish smiled even wider, then turned

for a look at her son. "I'll speak to Father Leary tomorrow and see about having the banns read at Mass."

"All right then," Sean said stiffly, "I'll leave it in your hands."

"Good. That's settled. Now," Ailish added, "you two don't mind me. I'll be in the car, Sean, whenever you're ready."

They watched her through the window to make sure she was all right, and once she was safely in the car again, Georgia grabbed his arm. "The priest? She's going to have the banns read in church?"

This was suddenly way more complicated. For three weeks running, the priest would read the names of the couples wanting to be married, giving anyone with a legal or civil objection a chance to speak up. But that just meant the news would fly around Dunley even faster than they'd expected.

He pushed one hand through his hair. "Aye, well, that's the way it's done, isn't it?"

"Can't you ask her to wait?"

"And use what for a reason?" He shook his head. "No, the banns will be read but it changes nothing. We'll still call it off when you break up with me. It'll all be fine, Georgia. You'll see." He grabbed her left hand and ran his thumb over her ring finger. "I'm sorry though, that I forgot about a ring."

"It isn't important."

His gaze locked with hers. "It is, and it'll be taken care of today. I'll see to it."

"Sean," she whispered, moving in close, then sliding a quick look at Ailish to make absolutely certain the woman couldn't overhear them, "are you really *sure* we're doing the right thing?"

"I am," he insisted, dipping his head to hers. "She's

tired, Georgia. I've never seen my mother so pale, and I've no wish to give her a setback right now. Let's see her up and moving around and back to herself before we end this. We have a deal, right?"

She sighed miserably. "We do."

"Good then." He kissed her hard and fast. "I'll just take mother to the manor house, then I'll come back and help you paint."

Surrendering, she smiled and asked, "Are you a good painter?"

"I'm a man of many talents," he reminded her.

And as he walked out of the shop, Georgia thought, he really hadn't needed to remind her of that at all.

Six

"I've an itch between my shoulder blades," Sean confessed the following day, as he followed Ronan into the front parlor of his cousin's house.

He felt as if he were surrounded by women lately. Ordinarily, not a bad thing at all. But just now, between Georgia and his mother and his housekeeper and even Laura, who was giving him a glare every time they met up, he was ready for some strictly male company. And his cousin was the one to understand how he was feeling. Or so he thought.

"Not surprising." Ronan walked to the corner, where an elegant table stood in for a bar, and headed for the small refrigerator that held the beer he and Sean both needed. "It's probably much what a rabbit feels when the hunter's got his gun trained on it."

Sean winced and glared at his cousin's back. "Thanks for that. I've come to you looking for solidarity and you turn on me like a snake. Are you going to be no comfort to me in this?"

"I won't." Ronan bent to the fridge, opened it and pulled out two beers. As he closed the door again, he spotted something small and white beside it on the floor and picked it up. "A shirt button?"

"What?"

"A shirt button," Ronan repeated, standing up and glancing down at his own shirt front as if expecting to see that one of the buttons had leaped free of the fabric. "Where did that come from?"

Sean knew exactly where. It was one of his, after all, torn from his shirt the first night he and Georgia had made love, right here in this room, before a roaring fire. At the thought of that, he went hard as stone and covered his discomfort by snapping, "How'm I to know why your shirt button is on the bloody floor? Did you not hear me, Ronan? I said I'm in trouble."

Frowning still at the button, Ronan tossed it onto the table, then crossed the room and handed one of the beers to Sean. "'Tis no more than you deserve," he said, tearing off the bottle cap and taking a long drink. "I warned you, didn't I, at my own bleeding wedding, to keep your hands off our Georgia?"

Sean uncapped his beer as well and took a long, thirsty drink. Ronan had indeed warned him off, but even now, when things had gotten so completely confused, he couldn't bring himself to regret ignoring that warning.

"When a man's tempted by a woman like her," Sean mused, "he's hard put to remember unwanted advice."

"And yet, when the shite hits the fan, you come to me for more of that advice."

Sean scowled at his cousin. He'd thought to find a little male solidarity here in this house that had been as much

his home as Ronan's since he was a child. Seems he'd
been wrong. "When you've done gloating, let me know."

"I'll be a while yet," Ronan mused and dropped onto
the sofa. Propping his booted feet up on the table in front
of him, he glanced up at Sean and said, "What's got you
so itchy, then?"

"What hasn't?" Shaking his head, Sean wandered the
room, unable to settle. Unable to clear his mind enough
to examine exactly why he felt as though he were doing
a fast step-toe dance on a hot skillet—barefoot.

"Then pick one out of the bunch to start with."

"Fine." Sean whirled around, back to the fire, to face
his cousin. Heat seared him from head to toe, and still
there was a tiny chill inside it couldn't reach. "Father
Leary dropped in on me this morning, wanting to have
a 'pre-marriage' chat."

Ronan snorted. "Aye, I had one with the old man, as
well. Always amazed me, bachelor priests thinking they
know enough about marriage to be handing out counsel
on how to treat a wife."

"Worse than that, he wanted to tell me all about how
sex with a wife is different from sex with a mistress."

Ronan choked on a sip of beer, then burst out laughing.
"That's what you get for having a reputation as quite the
ladies' man. Father didn't feel it necessary to warn me
of such things." As Ronan considered that, he frowned,
clearly wondering whether or not he should be insulted.

"Fine for you," Sean grumbled. "I don't know which
of us was more uncomfortable with that conversation—
me, or the good father himself."

"I'd bet on you."

"You'd win that one, all right," Sean said, then took
another drink of his beer. Shaking his head, he pushed

that confrontation with the village priest out of his head. "Then there's Katie—"

"Your housekeeper?"

"No, the other Katie in my life, of *course* my bloody housekeeper," Sean snapped. "She's buying up bridal magazines and bringing them to Mother, who's chortling over them as if she's planning a grand invasion. She's already talked to me about flowers, as if I know a rose from a daisy, and do we want to rent a canvas to stretch over the gardens for the reception in case of rain—"

"Shouldn't be news to you," Ronan said mildly. "Not the first time you've been engaged, after all."

"'Tisn't the same," Sean muttered.

"Aye, no, because that time it wasn't a game, was it? And when Noreen dumped your ass and moved on, you couldn't have cared less."

All true, Sean thought. He'd asked Noreen Callahan to marry him more than three years ago now. It had seemed, he considered now, the thing to do at the time. After all, Noreen was witty and beautiful, and she liked nothing better than going to all the fancy dos he was forced to attend as Irish Air made a name for itself.

But he hadn't put in the time. He'd spent every minute on his business, and finally Noreen had had enough. She'd come to understand that not even getting her mitts on Sean's millions was enough motivation to live with a man who barely noticed her existence.

Sean had hardly noticed when she left. So what did that say about him? He'd decided then that he wasn't the marrying sort and nothing yet had happened to change his mind.

"This was all your idea," Ronan reminded him.

"Do you think I don't know that?" He scrubbed one hand across his face, then pushed that hand through his hair, fingers stabbing viciously. The longer this lie went on, the more it evolved. "There's a pool at the Penny-whistle, you know. Picking out dates for the wedding *and* the birth of our first child."

"I've five euros on December twenty-third myself." Ronan studied the label on his bottle of Harp.

"Why the bloody hell would you do that? You *know* there's not to be a wedding!"

"And if I don't enter a pool about your wedding, don't you think those in the village would wonder why?"

"Aye, I suppose." Sean shook his head and looked out the window at the sunny afternoon. Shadows slid across the lawn like specters as the trees that made them swayed in the wind. "No one in the village was this interested in my life when it was Noreen who was the expected bride."

"Because no one in the village could stand the woman," Ronan told him flatly. "A more nose-in-the-air, preten-tious female I've never come across."

Hard to argue with that assessment, Sean thought, so he kept his mouth shut.

"But everyone around here *likes* Georgia. She's a fine woman."

"As if I didn't know that already."

"Just as you knew this would happen, Sean. It can't be a surprise to you."

"No, it's not," he admitted, still staring out the glass, as if searching for an answer to his troubles. "But it all feels as though it's slipping out of my control, and I've no idea how to pull it all back in again."

"You can't," Ronan said easily, and Sean wanted to kick him.

"Thanks for that, too." He sipped at his beer again and got no pleasure from the cold, familiar taste. "I'm seeing this whole marriage thing get bigger and bigger, and I've no idea what's going to happen when we finally call it off."

"Should've thought of that before this half-brained scheme of yours landed you in such a fix."

"Again, you're a comfort to me," he said, sarcasm dripping in his tone. "I've told Georgia I'll see to it that everyone blames me. But now I'm seeing that it's more complicated than that. Did you know, my assistant's already fielding requests for wedding invitations from some of my business associates?"

"Lies take on a life of their own," Ronan said quietly.

"True enough." Sean's back teeth clenched, as he remembered exactly how he'd gotten into this whole thing, and for the life of him, he couldn't say for sure now that he would have done it differently if given a chance. "You didn't see my mother lying in that hospital bed, Ronan. Wondering if she'd recover—or if, God forbid, I was going to lose her. Seeing her face so pale and then the tears on her cheeks as she worried for me." He paused and shook his head. "Scared me."

"Scared me, too," Ronan admitted. "Your mother's important to me, you know."

"I do know that." Sean took a deep breath, shook off the tattered remnants of that fear and demanded, "So out of your fondness for my mother, why not help save her son?"

"Ah no, lad. You're on your own in this."

"Thanks for that, as well."

"I will say that if Georgia ends up shedding one tear over what you've dragged her into," Ronan told him, "I will beat you bloody."

"I know that, too." Sean walked back and sat down beside Ronan. He kicked his feet up onto the table and rested his bottle of beer on his abdomen. "I'd expect nothing less."

"Well then, we're agreed." Ronan reached over and clinked the neck of his beer against Sean's. "You're in a hole that's getting deeper with every step you take, Sean. Mind you don't go in over your head."

As he drank to that discomforting toast, Sean could only think that Ronan was too late with this particular warning. He knew damn well he was already so deep, he couldn't see sky.

From Georgia's cottage kitchen downstairs came the incredible scent of potato-leek soup and fresh bread.

Georgia inhaled sharply, then sighed as she looked at her sister. "I think I'm going to keep Patsy here with me. You go on home to Ronan and have him cook for you."

"Never gonna happen," Laura told her on a laugh. "Besides, Patsy wouldn't leave now even if I wanted her to—which I don't—she's too crazy about Fiona."

Georgia looked down at the tiny baby cuddled in her arms and smiled wistfully. Milk-white skin, jet-black eyelashes lying in a curve on tiny, round cheeks. Wisps of reddish-brown hair and a tiny mouth pursed in sleep. A well of love opened in Georgia's heart, and she wondered how anything so young, so helpless, could completely change the look of the entire world in less than a month.

"Can't blame Patsy for that. I know I'm Fiona's aunt, but really, isn't she just beautiful?"

"I think so," Laura answered, and plopped down onto Georgia's new bed. "It's so huge, Georgia. The love I have for her is so immense. I just never knew anything could feel like this."

A trickle of envy wound its way around Georgia's heart before she recognized it, then banished it. She didn't begrudge her sister one moment of her happiness. But Georgia could admit, at least to herself, that she wished for some of the same for herself.

But maybe that just wasn't going to happen for her. The whole "husband and family" thing. A pang of regret sliced through her at that thought, but she had to accept that not everyone found love. Not everyone got to have their dreams come true. And sometimes, she told herself, reality just sucked.

"It's terrific," Georgia said, and jiggled the baby gently when she stirred and made a soft mewing sound. "You've got Ronan, Fiona, you're painting again..." As Georgia had given up on her design dreams to sell real estate, Laura had set aside her paints and easel in favor of practicality. Knowing that she'd rediscovered her art, had found the inspiration to begin painting again, made Georgia's heart swell. "I'm really happy for you, Laura."

"I know you are," her sister said. "I want *you* to be happy, too, you know."

"Sure I know. But I am happy," Georgia said, adding a smile to the words to really sell it. "Honest. I'm starting a new business. I'm moving to a new country. I've got a brand-new niece and a new home—what's not to be happy about?"

"I notice you didn't mention your new faux fiancé."

Georgia frowned a bit. "I don't *have* Sean."

"As far as the whole village of Dunley is concerned you do."

"Laura..." Georgia sighed a little, then crossed the bedroom and handed the baby back to her mother. She understood why her sister was concerned, but hearing about it all the time didn't help and it didn't change anything.

"All I'm saying is," Laura said, as she snuggled her

daughter close, "well, I don't really know what I'm saying. But the point is, I'm worried about you."

"Don't be."

"Oh, okay. All better." Laura blew out an exasperated breath. "I love Sean and all, but *you're* my sister, and I'm worried that this is going to blow up in your face. The whole village is counting on this wedding now. What happens when you call it off?"

Niggling doubts had Georgia chewing at her bottom lip. Hadn't she been concerned about the same thing from the very beginning? Everyone in Dunley was excited about the "wedding." Ailish had ordered a cake from the baker and then gleefully told Georgia that it was all taken care of.

"I don't know, but it's too late to worry about that now," she said firmly, and crossed the room to tug at the hem of the new curtains over one of the three narrow windows overlooking Sean's faery wood. A smile curved her mouth as she thought of him.

"I see that."

"What?"

"That smile. You're thinking about him."

"Stop being insightful. It's disturbing."

Laura laughed and shook her head. "Fine. I'll back off. For now."

"It's appreciated." Georgia didn't need her sister's worries crowding into her head. She barely had room for her own.

"So, do you need help packing?"

Now it was Georgia's turn to laugh. "For a trip I'm not taking until next week?"

"Fine, fine." Laura sighed a little. "I'm just trying to help out. I want you settled in and happy here, Georgia."

"I *am*." She looked around the bedroom of her new cottage.

It really helped knowing the owner, since Sean had given her the keys so she could move in *before* escrow closed on the place. It was good to have her own home, even though it wouldn't really feel like hers until she had some of her own furniture and things around her. Thank God, though, as a rental it had come furnished, so she at least had a place to sit and sleep, and pots and pans for the kitchen.

She'd taken the smaller of the two cottages Sean had shown her. The other one had been a row cottage, differentiated from the homes on either side of it only by the shade of emerald green painted on the front door. It was bigger and more modern, but the moment Georgia had seen *this* one, she'd been lost.

Mainly because this cottage appealed to her sense of whimsy.

It was a freestanding home, with a thatched roof and white-washed walls. Empty flower boxes were attached to the front windows like hope for spring. The door was fire-engine red, and the back door opened onto a tiny yard with a flower bed and a path that led into the faery wood.

The living room was small, with colorful rugs strewn across a cement floor that was painted a deep blue. A child-sized fireplace was tucked into one wall with two chairs pulled up in front of it. The kitchen was like something out of the forties, but everything worked beautifully. The staircase to the second floor was as steep as a ladder, and her bedroom was small with her bed snuggled under a sloping ceiling. But the windows looked out over the woods, and the bathroom had been updated recently to include a tub big enough to stretch out in.

It was a fairy-tale cottage, and Georgia already loved it.

This would be her first night in her new place, and she was anxious to nudge Laura on her way so that she could relax in that beautiful tub and pour herself a glass of wine to celebrate the brand-new chapter in her life.

"It is a great cottage." Laura looked at her for a long minute then frowned and asked, "You sure you don't want Fiona and me along for the trip back to California?"

"Absolutely not." On this, Georgia was firm. "I'm not going to be there for long, and all I have to do is sign the papers to put the condo up for sale. After that, when they find a buyer for the place, they can fax me the paperwork and I'll handle it from here. Then I'll arrange for my stuff to be shipped to Ireland and I'll be done. Besides," she added with a grim nod, "when I leave California, I'll be stopping in Ohio for the wedding."

Laura shook her head. "Why you're insisting on going to that is beyond me. I mean come on. You're over Mike, so what do you care?"

"I don't." And she realized as she said it that she really didn't care about her ex-husband and his soon-to-be wife, the husband-stealing former cheerleader. After all, if Mike hadn't been willing to cheat on his wife, Misty never would have gotten him in the first place.

So Georgia figured she was much better off without him anyway. "It's the principle of the thing, really. You know damn well Misty only sent me that tacky invitation to rub in my face that she and Mike are getting married. They never for a minute expect me to show up. So why shouldn't I? At the very least I should be allowed the pleasure of ruining their big day for them."

Laura chuckled. "I guess you're right. And seriously? Misty deserves to be miserable."

"She will be," Georgia promised with a laugh. "She's

marrying Mike, after all. May they be blessed with a dozen sons, every one of them just like their father."

"Wow," Laura said, obviously impressed, "you're really getting the hang of being Irish. A blessing and a curse all at the same time."

"It's a gift."

Georgia glanced down at her ring finger. She still wasn't entirely accustomed to the weight of the emerald and diamond ring Sean had given her for the length of their "engagement."

The dark green of the stone swam with color, and the diamonds winked in the light. It occurred to her then that while her new life was beginning with a lie—Mike was apparently *happy* with his. It didn't matter so much to her anymore, though Georgia could admit, if only to herself, that she'd spent far too much time wrapped up in anger and bitterness and wishing a meteor to crash down on her ex-husband's head.

It was irritating to have to acknowledge just how much time she had wasted and how much useless energy had been spent thinking about how her marriage had ended while the man who had made her so miserable wasn't suffering at all.

She had locked her heart away to avoid being hurt again, which was just stupid. She could see that now. Being hurt only meant that you were alive enough to feel it. And if her soul wasn't alive, then why bother going through the motions trying to pretend different? At least, she told herself, using her thumb against the gleaming gold band of the ring on her finger, she'd gotten past it, had moved on.

Then a voice inside her laughed. Sure, she'd moved on. To a ring that meant nothing and planning a fake future with a fake fiancé.

Wow. How had all of this happened anyway?

Still befuddled by her train of thought, she didn't notice Laura scooting off the bed until her sister was standing beside her.

"I should gather up Patsy and go," she said. "It's nearly time to feed Fiona, and Ronan's probably starving, as well."

Pleased at the idea of having some time to herself, Georgia lovingly nudged her sister to the door. "Go home. Feed the baby. Kiss your husband. I've got a lot to do around here before I leave for my trip next week. Don't worry, you'll have plenty of time to nag me before I leave. And then I'll be back before you even miss me."

"Okay." Laura gave her a one-armed hug and kissed her cheek. "Be careful. And for heaven's sake, take a picture of Misty's wedding gown. That's bound to be entertaining."

Laughing, Georgia vowed, "I will."

"And about Sean—"

"You said you were backing off."

"Right." Laura snapped her mouth shut firmly, took a breath and said, "Okay, then. Enjoy your new house and the supper Patsy left for you. Then have a great trip with your pretend fiancé and hurry home."

When her sister had gone down the stairs and she and Patsy had both shouted a goodbye, Georgia dropped onto the edge of her bed, relishing the sudden silence.

Home, she thought with a sigh. This cottage, in Dunley, Ireland, was now *home*.

It felt good.

She took a long bath, savored a glass of wine in the stillness, then dressed in what she thought of as her Ireland winter wear—jeans, sneakers and a shirt with one of her thick, cable-knit sweaters, this one a dark red, over it—and went downstairs.

Restless, she wandered through her new home, passing through the kitchen to break off a piece of the fresh bread Patsy had left for her. Walking back to the small living room, she paused in the center and did a slow turn.

There were still changes to be made, of course. She wouldn't bring all of her things from America, but the few items she loved would fit in here and make it all seem more *hers* somehow. Though already she felt more at home here than she ever had in the plush condo in Huntington Beach.

The fire in the hearth glowed with banked heat, its red embers shining into the room. Outside her windows, the world was dark as it could be only in the country. The streetlights of the village were a faint smudge in the blackness.

Georgia turned on the television. Then, the instant the sound erupted, turned it off again. She hugged herself and wished for company. Not the tinny, artificially cheerful voice of some unknown news anchor.

"Maybe I should get a dog," she mused aloud, listening to the sound of her own voice whisper into the stillness around her. She smiled at the thought of a clumsy puppy running through the cottage, and she promised herself that when she left America to come home to Dunley for good, she would find a puppy. She missed Beast. And Deidre. And the sound of Ronan's and Laura's voices. And the baby's cries. And Patsy's quiet singing when she was working in the kitchen.

She wanted another heartbeat in the house.

Georgia frowned as she realized the hard truth. What she wanted was Sean.

She could call him, of course, and actually started

for her phone before stopping again. Not a good idea to turn to him when she was lonely. He wouldn't always be there, right? Better she stand on her own, right from the beginning.

Plus, if she was making Dunley her home now, then she might as well get used to going about the village on her own. With that thought in mind, she snagged her jacket off the coat tree by the door and headed for the Pennywhistle.

It was a short walk from her door to the main street of the village, and from there only a bit more to the pub, but she fought for every step. The wind roared along the narrow track, pushing at Georgia and the few other hardy souls wandering the sidewalks with icy hands, as if trying to steer them all back to their homes.

Finally, though, she reached the pub, yanked open the heavy door and stepped into what felt like a *wall* of sound. The silence of the night was shattered by the rise and fall of conversations and laughter, the quick, energetic pulse of the traditional music flowing from the corner and the heavy stomp of booted feet dancing madly to the tune.

Just what I need, Georgia thought, and threw herself into the crush.

Seven

Georgia edged her way to the bar, slipping out of her jacket as she went. The heat inside was nearly stifling, what with the crowd of people and the fire burning merrily in the corner. Waitresses moved through the mob of people with the sort of deft grace ballet dancers would envy, carrying trays loaded with beer, whiskey, soft drinks and cups of tea.

A few people called hello to her as she made her way to the bar and Georgia grinned. This was just what she needed, she thought, to remind herself that she *did* have a real life; it merely also included a fake fiancé. She had friends here. She belonged, and that felt wonderful.

Jack Murphy, the postmaster, a man of about fifty with graying hair and a spreading girth, leaped nimbly off his stool at the bar and offered it to her. She knew better than to wave off his chivalry, though she felt a bit guilty for chasing him out of his seat.

"Thanks, Jack," she said, loud enough to be heard. "Looks like a busy night."

"Ah, well, on a cold night, what's better than a room full of friends and a pint?"

"Good point," she said, and, still smiling, turned to Danny Muldoon, the proprietor of the Pennywhistle.

A big man with a barrel chest, thinning hair and a mischievous smile, he had a bar towel slung over one shoulder and a clean white apron strung around his waist. He was manning the beer taps like a concert pianist as he built a Guinness with one hand and poured a Harp with another. He glanced up at her and asked, "Will it be your usual then, love?"

Her usual.

She loved that. "Yes, Danny, thanks. The Chardonnay when you get a minute."

He laughed, loud and long. "That'll be tomorrow morning by the looks of this crowd, but I'll see you put right as soon as I've finished with this."

Georgia nodded and turned on her stool to look over the crowd. With her jacket draped across her knees, she studied the scene spread out in front of her. Every table was jammed with glassware, every chair filled, and the tiny cleared area closest to the musicians was busy with people dancing to the wild and energetic tunes being pumped out furiously by a fiddle, a flute and a bodhran drum. Georgia spotted Sinead's husband, Michael, and watched as he closed his eyes and tapped his foot to the reel spinning from his fiddle. Sinead sat close by, her head bent to the baby in her arms as she smiled to the music her husband and his friends made.

Here was Dunley, Georgia thought. Everyone was welcome in Irish pubs. From the elderly couple sitting together and holding hands to the tiny girl trying to step-dance like her mother, they were all here. The village. The sense of community was staggering. They were part of each other's lives. They had a connection, one to the other, and the glorious part of it all, in Georgia's mind, was that they had included *her* in their family.

When the incredibly fast-paced song ended, the music slid into a ballad, the notes of which tugged at Georgia's heart. Then one voice in the crowd began to sing and was soon joined by another until half the pub was singing along.

She turned and saw her wine waiting for her and Georgia lifted it for a sip as she listened to the song and lost herself in the beauty of the moment.

She was so caught up, she didn't even notice when Sean appeared at her side until he bent his head and kissed her cheek.

"You've a look of haunted beauty about you," he whispered, and Georgia's head spun briefly.

She turned and looked up at him. "It's the song."

"Aye, 'The Rising of the Moon' is lovely."

"What's it about?"

He winked and grinned. "Rebellion. What we Irish do best."

That song ended on a flourish, and the musicians basked in applause before taking a beer break.

"What'll it be for you then, Sean?" Danny asked.

"A Jameson's if you please, Danny. *Tá sé an diabhal an oíche fuar féin.*"

"It is indeed," the barman answered with a laugh.

"What was that?" Georgia asked. "What did you say?"

Sean shrugged, picked up his glass and laid money down for both his and Georgia's drinks. "Just a bit of the Gaelic. I said it's the devil's own cold night."

"You speak *Gaelic?*"

"Some," he said.

Amazing. Every time she thought she knew him, she found something new. And this was touching, she thought. "It sounds…musical."

"We've music in us, that's for sure," Sean acknowledged. "A large part of County Mayo is Gaeltacht, you know. That means 'Irish-speaking.' Most of those who live here have at least a small understanding of the language. And some speak it at home as their first language."

She'd heard snippets of Gaelic since she first came to Ireland, but it had never occurred to her that it was still a living language. And, to be honest, some of the older people here spoke so quickly and had such thick accents, at first she'd thought they were speaking Gaelic—though it was English.

"Of course," she said after a sip of wine. "The aisle signs in the grocery store are in both English and Gaelic. And the street signs. I just thought maybe it was for the tourists, you know…"

He tapped one finger to her nose. "It's for us. The Irish language was near lost not so very long ago. After the division and the Republic was born, the government decided to reclaim all we'd nearly lost. Now our schools teach it and our children will never have to worry about losing a part of who they are."

Georgia just looked at him. There was a shine of pride in his eyes as he spoke, and she felt a rush of something warm and delicious spread through her in response.

"We're a small country but a proud one," he went on, staring down into his glass of whiskey. "We hang on to what we have and fight when another tries to take it." He shot a quick look at the man on the stool beside Georgia. "Isn't that so, Kevin Dooley?"

The man laughed. "I've fought you often enough for a beer or a woman or just for the hell of it."

"And never won," Sean countered, still grinning.

"There's time yet," Kevin warned companionably, then smiled and turned back to his conversation.

Georgia laughed, too, then leaned into Sean as the musicians picked up their instruments again and the ancient pub came alive with music that filled the heart and soul. With Sean's arm around her, Georgia allowed herself to be swept into the magic of the moment.

And she refused to remember, at least for tonight, that Sean was only hers temporarily.

Two hours later, Sean walked her to the cottage and waited on the step while she opened the door. Georgia went inside, then paused and looked at him.

For the first time in days, they were alone together. With his mother recuperating at his house and her at Ronan and Laura's, they'd been able to do little more than smile at each other in passing.

Until tonight.

Earlier that night, she'd been wishing for him and now, here he was.

He stood in the doorway, darkness behind him, lamplight shining across his face, defining the desire quickening in his eyes. The cold night air slipped inside, twisted with the heat from the banked fire and caused Georgia to shiver in response.

"Will you invite me in, Georgia?"

Her heartbeat sped up, and her mouth went dry. There was something about this man that reached her on levels she hadn't even been aware of before knowing him. He'd made a huge difference in her life, and she was only now realizing how all-encompassing that difference was.

Just now, just this very minute, she stared up at Sean and felt everything within her slide into place, like jagged puzzle pieces finally creating the picture they were meant to be.

There was more here, she thought, than a casual affair. There was affection and danger and excitement and a bone-deep knowledge that when her time with Sean was done, she'd never be the same again.

It was far too late to pull back, she thought wildly. And though she knew she'd be hurt when it was all over, she wouldn't have even if she could.

Because what she'd found with Sean was what she'd been looking for her whole life.

She'd found out who she was.

And more importantly, she *liked* the woman she'd discovered.

"Is it so hard then, to welcome me into your home?" Sean asked softly, when her silence became too much for him.

"No," she said, reaching out to grab hold of his shirtfront. She dragged him inside, closed the door then went up on her toes. "It's not hard at all," she said, and then she kissed him.

At the first long taste of him, that wildness inside her softened. Her bones seemed to melt until she was leaning into him, the only thing holding her up was the strength of Sean's arms wrapped around her.

Her body went up like a torch. Heat suffused her, swamping Georgia with a need so deep, so all-consuming, she could hardly draw breath. When he tore his mouth from hers, she groaned.

"You've a way about you, Georgia," he whispered, dipping his head to nibble at her ear.

She shivered and tipped her head to one side, giving

him easier access. "I was just thinking the same thing about you…" She sighed a little. "Oh, that feels so good."

"You taste of lemons and smell like heaven."

Georgia smiled as her eyes closed and she gave herself up to the sensations rattling through her. "I had a long soak in that wonderful tub upstairs."

"Sorry to have missed that," he murmured, dragging his lips and tongue and teeth along the line of her neck until she quivered in his arms and trembled, incredibly on the brink of a climax. Just his touch. Just the promise of what was to come was enough to send her body hurtling toward completion.

The man had some serious sexual power.

"I thought about you today," he whispered, turning her to back her up against the front door. He lifted his head, looked her dead in the eye and fingered her hair as he spoke. "Thought I'd lose my mind at the office today, trying to work out the figures on the new planes we've ordered… Galway city never seemed so far from Dunley before." He dropped his hands to her waist, pulled up the hem of her sweater and tugged at the snap of her jeans. "And all I could think about was you. Here. And finally having you all to myself again."

The brush of his knuckles against the bare skin of her abdomen sent a zip of electricity shooting through her veins. Releasing him long enough to shrug out of her jacket, she let it fall to the floor, unheeded.

"You're here now," she told him, reaching up to push his jacket off, as well. He helped her with that, then went back to the waistband of her jeans and worked the zipper down so slowly she wanted to scream.

"I am," he said, dipping his head for a kiss. "And so're you."

He had the fly of her jeans open, and he slid one hand

down across her abdomen, past the slip of elastic on her panties and down low enough to touch the aching core of her.

The moment his hand cupped her, she shattered. She couldn't stop it. Didn't want to. She had been primed and ready for his touch for days. Georgia cried out and rocked her hips into his hand. While her body trembled and shook, he kissed her, whispering bits and pieces of Gaelic that seemed to slide into her heart. He stroked her, his fingers dipping into her heat while she rode his hand feverishly, letting the ecstasy she'd found only with him take her up and then under.

When it was done and she could breathe again, she looked up into his eyes and found him watching her with a hunger she'd never seen before. His passion went deeper and gleamed more darkly in his eyes. He held her tenderly, as if she were fragile and about to splinter apart.

"Shatter tú liom," he said softly, gaze moving over her face like a touch.

Still trying to steady her breathing, she reached up to cup his cheek in her palm. The flash of her ring caught her eye but she ignored it. This wasn't fake, she thought. This, what she and Sean shared when they were together, was *very* real. She had no idea what it meant—and maybe it didn't have to *mean* anything. Maybe it was enough to just shut off her mind and enjoy what she had while she had it.

"What does that mean?"

He turned his face into her palm and kissed her. "'You shatter me,' that's what I said."

Her heartbeat jolted, and a sheen of unexpected tears welled up in her eyes, forcing her to blink them back before she could make a fool of herself and cry.

"I watch you tremble in my arms and you take my

knees out from under me, Georgia. That's God's truth." He kissed her, hard, fast, and made her brain spin. "What you do to me is nothing I've ever known before."

She knew exactly what he meant because she felt the same. What she had with Sean was unlike any previous relationship. Sometimes, she felt as though she were stumbling blindly down an unfamiliar road and the slightest misstep could have her falling off a cliff. How could anything feel so huge? How could it not be real? And still, this journey was one she wouldn't have missed for anything.

"Say something else," she urged. "In Gaelic, say something else."

He gave her a smile and whispered, *"Leat mo anáil uaidh."*

She returned his smile. "Now translate."

"'You take my breath away.'"

To disguise the quick flash of feelings too deep to explore at the moment, Georgia quipped, "Back atcha. That means 'same to you.'"

He chuckled, rested his forehead against hers, pulled his hand from her jeans and wrapped both arms around her. "I've got to have you, Georgia. It feels like years since I've felt your skin against mine. You're a hunger in me, and I'm a starving man."

Her stomach did a fast roll and her heartbeat leaped into a gallop. And still she teased him because she'd discovered she liked the teasing, flirtatious way they had together. "Starving? Patsy Brennan left some bread and soup in the kitchen."

"You're a hard woman," he said, but the curve of his mouth belied the words.

"Or," she invited, taking his hand in hers and heading

for the stairs, "you can come up with me and we'll find something else to ease your appetite."

"Lá nó oíche, Tá mé do fear."

She stopped and looked at him. "Now you're just doing that because you know what it does to me."

"I am indeed."

"What did you say that time?"

"I am indeed."

Her lips quirked at the humor in his eyes. "Funny. Before that, what did you say?"

"I said," he told her, swooping in to grab her close and hold on tight like a drowning man clinging to the only rope in a stormy sea, "'Day or night, I'm your man.'"

Then his mouth came down on hers and every thought but one dissolved.

Her man. Those two words repeated over and over again in her mind while Sean was busy kissing her into oblivion. He was hers. For now. For tonight. For however long they had together.

And that was going to have to be enough.

When he let her up for air, she held his hand and shakily led the way up the steep flight of stairs. The ancient treads groaned and squeaked beneath them, but it was a cozy sound. Intimate. At the head of the stairs, Georgia pulled Sean into her room and then turned to look up at him.

He glanced around the bedroom and smiled as he noted everything she'd done to it. "You've made it nice in here. In just a day."

She followed his gaze, noting the fresh curtains at the windows, the quilt on the bed and the colorful pillows tossed against the scrolled iron headboard.

"Laura and Patsy brought a few things over from the manor."

"You've made it a home already."

"I love it already, too," she confessed. "And when I get some of my own things in here, it'll be perfect."

"'Tis perfect right now," he said, moving in on her with a stealthy grace that made her insides tremble. "There's a bed after all."

"So there is."

"I've a need to have you stretched across that bed," he told her, undoing the buttons of his shirt so he could tear it off and throw it onto a nearby chair. "I've a need to touch every square inch of that luscious body of yours and then, when I've finished, to begin again."

Georgia drew a long, unsteady breath and yanked her sweater up and off, before throwing it aside with Sean's shirt. Her fingers were shaky as she tugged at the buttons on her blouse, but Sean's hands were suddenly there, making fast work of them. Then he pushed the fabric off her shoulders and let it slide down her arms to puddle on the floor.

Outside, the night was clear for a change. No rain pinged against the windows, but moonlight did a slow dance through the glass. Inside, the house was still, only the sounds of their ragged breathing to disturb the quiet.

Georgia couldn't hear anything over the pounding of her own heart, anyway. Sean undid the front clasp of her bra, and she slipped out of it eagerly. His hands at her waist, her hands at his, and he pushed her jeans down her hips as she undid the hook and zipper of his slacks, then pushed them down, as well.

In seconds they were naked, the rest of their clothes discarded as quickly as possible. Georgia threw herself into his arms, and when he lifted her off her feet she felt a thrill in her bones. He tucked her legs around his waist, and she hooked her ankles together at the small of his back.

He took two long steps to the nearest wall and braced her back against it. With her arms around his neck, she looked down into his eyes and said breathlessly, "I thought we needed the bed."

"And so we will," he promised. "When we're too tired to stand."

Then he entered her. His hard, thick length pushing into her welcoming body. Georgia could have sworn he went deep enough to touch the bottom of her heart. She felt him all through her, as if he'd laid claim to her body and soul and was only now letting her in on it.

The wall was cold against her back, but she didn't feel it. All she was aware of was the tingling spread of something miraculous inside her. Her body was spiraling into that coil of need that would tighten until it burst from the pressure and sent jagged shards of sensation rippling through her.

Bracing one hand on the dresser beside her, Georgia clapped the other to his shoulder and moved with him as he set a frenetic pace. She watched his eyes glaze over, saw the mix of pleasure and tension etch themselves onto his features. Again and again he took her, pushing her higher and higher, faster and faster.

Her heels dug into his back, urging him on, and when the first hard jolt of release slammed into her, she shouted his name and clung desperately to him. She was still riding the ripples of her climax when he buried his face in the curve of her neck and joined her there.

A few miles away at Laura's house, the phone rang and Laura picked it up on the run. She had just gotten the baby down for the night and she had a gorgeous husband waiting for her in the front parlor with a bottle of wine.

"Hello?"

"Laura, love," Ailish said. "And how's our darling Fiona this night?"

Sean's mother. Why was she calling? Did she suspect something? *This* was why Laura didn't like lies. They tangled everything up. Made her unsure what she could say and what she couldn't. Sean and Georgia were trying to protect Ailish, and what if Laura said something that blew the whole secret out of the water? What if she caused Ailish a heart attack? What if—

Laura stepped into the parlor, gave her husband a silent *Oh Dear God* look and answered, "The baby's wonderful, Ailish. I've just put her down."

"Lovely, then you have a moment?"

"Um, sure," she said desperately, "but wouldn't you like to say hello to Ronan?"

At that, her devoted husband shot out of his chair, shaking his head and waving both hands.

Laura scowled at him and mouthed the word *coward*.

He bowed at the waist, accepting the insult as if it were a trophy.

"No, dear, this is better between us, I think," Ailish told her through the phone.

Uh-oh. She didn't want to talk to Ronan? *Better between us?* That couldn't be good.

Deserted by the man she loved, Laura took a breath and waited for the metaphorical ax to fall.

"I just want to ask you one question."

No, no, no. That wasn't a good idea at all.

"Oh!" Laura interrupted her frantically, with one last try for escape. "Wait! I think I hear Fiona—"

"No, you don't. And there's no point trying to lie to me, Laura Connolly. You've no talent for it, dear."

It was the Irish way. A compliment and a slap all in the same sentence.

"Yes, ma'am," she said, throwing a trapped look at her husband. Ronan only shrugged and poured each of them a drink. When he was finished, he handed her the wine and Laura took a long gulp.

"Now then," Ailish said and Laura could picture the tiny, elegant woman perfectly. "I know my son, and I've a feeling there's more going on between him and Georgia than anyone is telling me."

"I don't—"

"No point in lying, Laura dear, remember?"

She sighed.

"That's better." Then to Sean's housekeeper, Ailish said, "Thank you, Katie. A cup of tea would be wonderful. And perhaps one or two of your scones? Laura and I are just settling down for a long chat."

Oh, God, Laura thought. A long chat? That wasn't good. Wasn't good at all. Quickly, she drained her glass and handed it to her husband for a refill.

Eight

For the entire next week, Sean felt that itch between his shoulder blades. And every day, it got a little sharper. A little harder to ignore. Everywhere he went, people in the village were talking about the upcoming wedding. It shouldn't have bothered him, as he'd known full well what would happen the moment he began this scheme. But knowing it and living it were two different things.

The pool in the pub was more popular than ever—with odds changing almost daily as people from outlying farms came in to make their bets on the date of the wedding. Even the Galway paper had carried an engagement announcement, he thought grimly, courtesy of Ailish.

From her sickbed, his mother had leaped into the planning of this not-to-be wedding with such enthusiasm, he shuddered to think what she might do once she was cleared by her doctor.

When the article in the paper had come out, it had

taken Sean more than an hour of fast talking with Georgia to smooth that particular bump in the road. She was less and less inclined to keep up the pretense as time went by, and even Sean was beginning to doubt the wisdom of the whole thing.

But then, he would see his mother moving slowly through the house and tell himself that he'd done the right thing. The only thing. Until Ailish was well and fit again, he was going to do whatever he had to.

Though to accomplish it, the annoying itch would become his constant companion.

Even Ronan and Laura had been acting strangely the past few days, Laura especially. She had practically sequestered herself in the manor, telling Georgia she was simply too exhausted with caring for the baby to be good company.

Frowning, Sean told himself there was definitely something going on there, but he hadn't a clue what it was. Which made this trip with Georgia to the States seem all the more attractive.

At the moment, getting away from everyone in Ireland for a week or so sounded like a bloody vacation. Going to California to close out Georgia's house and then on to Ohio, of all places, for the wedding, would give both of them a chance to relax away from the stress of the lies swarming around them like angry bees.

Or maybe it was the muted roar of the plane's engines making him think of swarming bees. He and Georgia had the jet to themselves for this trip, but for the pilots and Kelly, the flight attendant who had already brought them coffee right after takeoff and then disappeared into the front of the jet, giving them privacy.

He looked at Georgia, sitting across from him, and Sean felt that quick sizzle of heat and need that he'd become accustomed to feeling whenever he was close to her. Oh, since the moment he first met her at Ronan's wedding, he had felt the zing of attraction and interest any man would feel for a woman like Georgia.

But in the past few weeks, that zing had become something else entirely. He spent far too much time thinking about her. And when he was with her, he kept expecting to feel the edge of his need slackening off as it always had before with the women he was involved with. It hadn't happened, of course. Instead, that need only became sharper every time he was with her. As if feeding his hunger for her only defined his appetite, not quenched it.

It wasn't just the sex, either, he mused, studying her profile in the clear morning light. He liked the way her short, honey-blond hair swung at her chin. He liked the deep twilight of her eyes and how they darkened when he was inside her. He liked her sense of style—the black skirt, scooped-neck red blouse and the high heels that made her legs look bloody amazing. And he liked her mind. She had a quick wit, a sharp temper and a low tolerance for bullshit—all of which appealed to him.

She was on his mind all the bloody time and he couldn't say he minded it overmuch. The only thing that *did* bother him was the nagging sensation that he was coming to care for her more than he'd intended. Sean knew all too well that a man in love lost all control over a situation with his woman, and he wasn't a man who enjoyed that. He'd seen enough of his friends become fools over women. Even Ronan had lost a part of himself when he first tumbled for Laura.

No, Sean preferred knowing exactly what was happening and when, rather than being tossed about on a tide of emotion you couldn't really count on anyway.

And still…

There was a voice inside him whispering that perhaps *real* love was worth the risk. He argued that point silently as he'd no wish to find out.

A knot of something worrisome settled into the pit of his stomach and he determinedly chose to ignore it. No point in examining feelings at the moment anyway, was there? Right now, he was just going to enjoy watching her settle into the plush interior of one of his jets.

Her gaze didn't settle, but moved over the inside of the plane, checking out everything, missing nothing. Another thing to admire about her. She wasn't a woman to simply accept her surroundings. Georgia had enough curiosity to explore them. And Sean could admit that he wanted her opinion of his jets.

He was proud of what he'd built with Irish Air and had a million ideas for how to grow and expand the company. By the time he was finished, when someone thought luxury travel, he wanted Irish Air to be the name that came to mind.

"What do you think?" Sean had noticed how she had tensed up during takeoff, but now that they were at a cruising altitude, she was relaxed enough to ease her white-knuckled grip on the arms of the seat.

"Of the jet? It's great," she said. "Really beats flying coach."

"Should be our new slogan," Sean said, with a chuckle. "I'm glad you like it. Irish Air is a luxury airline. There are no coach seats. Everyone is a first-class passenger."

"A great idea, but I'm sure most of us couldn't afford to travel like this."

"It's not so dear as you'd think," Sean said. In fact, he'd made a point of doing as much as he could to keep the price down.

He was proud of what he'd built, but curious what

Georgia thought of his flagship. This plane was the one he used most often himself. But all of the others in his fleet were much like it.

Sean's idea had been to outfit a smaller plane with luxury accommodations. To give people who wouldn't ordinarily fly first class a chance to treat themselves. And yes, the price was a bit higher than coach, but still substantially less than that of a first-class ticket on an ordinary airline.

"It's cheaper than chartering a jet."

"Yeah," she said, flicking a curtain aside to take a look out the window at the clouds beneath them. "But coach is still way cheaper."

"You get what you pay for, don't you?" he asked, leaning back in his own seat to sip at his coffee. "When you fly Irish Air, your vacation begins the moment you board. You're treated like royalty. You arrive at your destination rested instead of wild-eyed and desperate for sleep."

"Oh, I get it," she said. "Believe me. And it's a great idea…"

He frowned as she left that thought hanging. *"But?"*

Georgia shot him a half grin. "But, okay." She set her coffee on the table. "You say your airline's different. Set apart."

"I do."

"But, inside, it's set up just like every other plane. A center aisle, seats on either side."

There was a shine in her eyes and Sean was paying more attention to that, than he was to her words. When what she'd said at last computed, he asked, "And how else should we have it arranged?"

"Well, that's the beauty of it, isn't it?" she countered. "It's your plane, Sean. You want to make Irish Air different from the crowd, so why even have them furnished like everyone else?"

She ran the flat of her hand across the leather arm rest and for a second, he allowed himself to picture that hand stroking him, instead. As his body tightened, he reminded himself they had a six-hour flight to New York and then another five to L.A. Plenty of time to show Georgia the owner's bedroom suite at the back of the jet. That brought a smile to his face, until he realized that Georgia was frowning thoughtfully.

"What is it you're thinking? Besides the fact that the seats are arranged wrong?"

"Hmm? Oh, nothing."

"It's something," he said, following her gaze as she studied the furnishings of the plane with a clearly critical eye. "Let's have it."

"I was just thinking…you say you started Irish Air as a way of giving people a real choice in flying."

"That's right," he said, leaning forward, bracing his elbows on his knees. "As I said, most can't afford first-class tickets on commercial airlines, and chartering a jet is well beyond them, as well. Irish Air," he said with a proud smile, "is in the buffer zone. I offer luxury travel for just a bit more than coach."

"How much is a bit?"

"More than a little," he hedged, "less than a lot. The theory being, if people save for an important vacation, then they might be willing to save a bit more to start their vacation the moment they board the plane." Warming to his theme, he continued. "You see, you fly coach, say from L.A. to Ireland. By the time you've arrived, you feel as though you've been dragged across a choppy sea. You're tired, you're angry, you're hungry. Then you've to rent a car and drive on a different side of the road when you're already on the ragged edge…"

"All true. I've done it," she said.

He nodded. "But, on Irish Air, you step aboard and you relax. There are fewer seats. The seats are wider, fold out into beds and there's a TV at every one of them. We offer WiFi on board and we serve *real* meals with actual knives and forks. When you arrive at your destination, you're rested, refreshed and feel as though your worries are behind you."

"You should do commercials," Georgia said with a smile. "With the way you look, that accent of yours and the way your eyes shine when you talk about Irish Air, you'd have women by the thousands lined up for tickets."

"That's the idea." He sat back, rested one foot on his opposite knee and glanced around. "By this time next year, Irish Air will be the most talked-about airline in the world. We'll be ordering a dozen new planes soon and—" He broke off when he saw her shift her gaze to one side and chew at her bottom lip. A sure sign that she had something to say and wasn't sure how to do it. "What is it?"

"You want the truth?"

"Absolutely," he told her.

"Okay, you want Irish Air to stand out from the crowd, right?"

"I do."

"So why are you creating such boring interiors?"

"What? Boring, did you say?" He glanced around the main cabin, saw nothing out of line and looked back at her for an explanation.

She half turned in her seat to face him, then slapped one hand against the armrest. "First, I already told you, the arrangement of the seats. There are only ten of them on this plane, but you've got them lined up in standard formation, with the aisle up the middle."

One eyebrow winged up. "There's a better way?"

"There's a *different* way, and that is what you said you wanted."

"True. All right then, tell me what you mean."

A light burned in her eyes as she gave him a quick grin. Unbuckling her seat belt, she stood up, looked down the length of the plane, then back to him.

"Okay. It's not just the seats," she said, "the colors are all wrong."

A bit insulted, as he'd paid a designer a huge sum to come up with a color palette that was both soothing and neutral, he asked, "What the bloody hell is wrong with beige?"

She shook her head sadly. "It's *beige,* Sean. Could any color be more ordinary?"

"I've had it on good authority that beige is calming and instills a sense of trust in the passenger."

"Who told you that?" she asked, tipping her head to one side as she studied him. "A man?"

He scowled. "I'm a man, if you've forgotten."

She gave him a wicked smile. "That's one thing I'm certain of."

He stood up, too, but she skipped back a pace to keep some distance between them. "*But* you're not a designer."

"I'm not, no." Considering, thinking, he watched her and said, "All right, then. Tell me what it is you're thinking, Georgia."

"Okay…" She took a breath and said, "First, the carpeting. It looks like the kind you see in a dentist's office. Trust me when I say *that* is not soothing."

He frowned thoughtfully at the serviceable, easy-to-clean carpet.

"It should be plush. Let a passenger's feet sink into it when they step on board." She wagged a finger at him. "Instant luxurious feel and people *will* notice."

"Thick carpet."

"Not beige," she added quickly. "I think blue. Like the color of a summer sky."

"Uh-huh."

She ran one hand across the back of the leather seat again. "These are comfortable, but again. Beige. Really?"

"You recommend blue again?" he asked, enjoying the animation on her face.

"No, for the seats, gray leather." She looked up at him. "The color of the fog that creeps in from the ocean at night. It'll go great with the blue carpet and it'll be different. Make Irish Air stand out from the crowd. And—" She paused as if she were wondering if she'd already gone too far.

He crossed his arms over his chest. "Go on, no reason to stop now."

"Okay, don't line the seats up like bored little soldiers. Clump them."

"Clump?"

"Yeah," she said. "In conversational groups. Like seats on a train. You said this is the midsize jet, right? So your others are even wider. Make use of that space. Make the interior welcoming. Two seats facing back, two forward. And stagger them slightly too, so the people sitting on the right side of the plane aren't directly opposite those on the left. Not everyone wants strangers listening in to conversations."

She walked down the aisle and pointed. "Have the last two back here, separate from the others. A romantic spot that seems cozy and set apart."

He looked at the configuration of his jet and in his

mind's eye, pictured what she was describing. He liked it. More, he could see that she was right. He'd seen the same sort of design on private corporate jets, of course, but not on a passenger line. Offering that kind of difference would help set Irish Air apart. The congenial airline. The jets that made travel a treat. And gray seats on pale blue carpet would look more attractive than the beige. Why hadn't he thought of that?

Better yet, why hadn't the "expert" he'd hired to design the interiors thought of it?

"Oh, and I hate those nasty little overhead light beams on airplanes. It's always so hard to arrow them down on what you want to read." Georgia looked at the slope of the walls, then back to him. "You could have small lamps attached to the hull. Like sconces. Brass—no, pewter. To go with the gray seats and offset the blue."

She reached down and lifted a table that was folded down into itself. Opening it, she pointed to the space on the wall just above. "And here, a bud vase, also affixed to the hull, with fresh flowers."

Sean liked it. Liked all of it. And the excitement in her eyes fired his own.

"Oh, and instead of the standard, plastic, pull-down shades on the windows, have individual drapes." She leaned over and put her hands to either side of one of the portholes. "Tiny, decorative curtain rods—also pewter—and a square of heavy, midnight-blue fabric…"

Before he could comment on that, she'd straightened up and walked past him to the small galley area. The flight attendant was sitting in the cockpit with the pilot and copilot, so there was no one in her way as she explored the functional kitchen setup.

She stepped out again and studied the wall with a

flat-screen television attached to it. "The bathroom is right here, yes?"

"One of them," he said. "There's another in the back."

"So, if you get rid of the big TV—and you should have individual screens at the seating clumps—and expand the bathroom wall another foot or so into the cabin," she took another quick look around the corner at the galley. "That gives you a matching extra space in the kitchen. And that means you could expand your menu. Offer a variety of foods that people won't get anywhere else."

He could bloody well see it, Sean thought. Frowning, he studied the interior of the jet and saw it not as it was now, but as it could be. As it *would* be, he told himself, the moment they got back to Ireland and he could fire the designer who'd suggested ordinary for his *extraordinary* airline.

Following Georgia's train of thought was dizzying, but the woman knew what she was talking about. She painted a picture a blind man could see and appreciate. Why she'd wasted her talent on selling houses, he couldn't imagine.

"You could even offer cribs for families traveling with babies." She was still talking. "If you bolt it down in the back there and have, I don't know, a harness or something for the baby to wear while it sleeps, that gives the mom a little time to relax, too."

He was nodding, making mental notes, astonished at the flow of brilliant ideas Georgia had. "You've a clever mind," he said softly. "And an artist's eye."

She grinned at him and the pleasure in her eyes was something else a blind man could see.

"What's in the back of the plane, through that door?" she asked, already headed toward it.

"Something I'd planned to show you later," he told her with a wink. Then he took her hand and led her down the narrow, ordinary aisle between boring beige seats. Opening the door, he ushered her inside, then followed her and closed the door behind them.

"You have a bedroom on your jets?" she asked, clearly shocked at the sight of the double bed, bedecked with a dark blue duvet and a half-dozen pillows. The shades were drawn over the windows, filling the room with shadow. Georgia looked up at him, shaking her head.

"This plane is mine," Sean told her. "I use it to fly all over the damn place for meetings and such, and so I want a place to sleep while I travel."

"And the seats that fold into beds aren't enough for you?"

"Call it owner's privilege," he said, walking closer, steadily urging her backward until the backs of her knees hit the edge of the mattress and she plopped down. Swinging her hair back from her face, she looked up at him.

"And do you need help designing this room, too?" she asked, tongue firmly in cheek.

"If I did, I now know who to call," he assured her.

"Does that door have a lock on it?" she asked, sliding her gaze to the closed door and then back to him.

"It does."

"Why don't you give it a turn, then?"

"Another excellent idea," Sean said, and moved to do just that.

Then he looked down at her and was caught by her eyes. The twilight shine of them. The clever mind behind them. Staring into her eyes was enough to mesmerize a man, Sean thought. He took a breath and dragged the scent of her into his lungs, knowing that air seemed empty without her scent flavoring it.

Slowly, she slipped her shoes off, then lay back on the mattress, spreading her arms wide, so that she looked like a sacrifice to one of the old gods. But the welcoming smile on her face told him that she wanted him as much as he did her.

In seconds, then, he was out of his clothes and helping her off with hers. The light was dim in the room, but he saw all he needed to see in her eyes. When he touched her, she arched into him and a sigh teased a smile onto her lips.

"Scáthanna bheith agat," he whispered. Amazing how often he felt the old language well up inside him when he was with her. It seemed only Irish could help him say what he was feeling.

She swept her fingers through his hair and said, "I love when you speak Gaelic. What did you say that time?"

"I said, 'Shadows become you,'" he told her, then dipped his head for a kiss.

"You make my heart melt sometimes, Sean," she admitted, her voice little more than a hush of sound.

That knot in his guts tightened further as words he might have said, but wouldn't, caught in his throat. Right now, more words were unnecessary anyway, he told himself.

Instead, he kissed her again, taking his time, tasting her, tangling his tongue with hers until neither of them were thinking. Until all either of them felt was the need for each other. He would take his time and savor every luscious inch of her. Indulge them both with a slow loving that would ease away the ragged edges they had been living with and remind them both how good they were together.

Well, Georgia told herself later that night, Sean was right about one thing. Flying Irish Air did deliver you to your destination feeling bright-eyed and alert. Of course, great sex followed by a nap on a real bed probably hadn't hurt, either.

Now Sean was out picking up some dinner, and she was left staring into her closet trying to decide what to pack, what to give away and what to toss.

"Who'm I trying to kid?" she asked aloud. "I'm taking my clothes with me. All of 'em."

She glanced at the stack of packing boxes on the floor beside her and sighed. Then her gaze moved around her bedroom in the condo she and Laura used to share.

She'd had good times in this house. Sort of surprising, too, since when she'd arrived here to move in with her sister, she hadn't really been in a good place mentally. Marriage dissolved, bank account stripped and ego crushed, she'd slowly, day by day, rebuilt a life for herself.

"And now," she whispered, "I'm building another."

"Talking to yourself? Not a good sign."

She whirled around to find Sean standing in the open doorway, holding a pizza box that smelled like heaven while he watched her with amusement glittering in his eyes.

In self-defense, she said, "I have to talk to myself, since I'm the only one who really understands me."

"*I* understand you, Georgia."

"Is that right?" She turned her back on the closet, the boxes and everything she had to do. Snatching the pizza box from him, she headed out of the bedroom and walked toward the stairs. He was right behind her. "Well then, why don't you tell me what I'm thinking?"

"Easily enough done," he said, his steps heavy on the stairs behind her. "You're excited, but worried. A bit embarrassed for having me catch you doing a monologue in your bedroom and you're hoping you've some wine in the kitchen to go with that pizza."

She looked over her shoulder at him and hoped the surprise she felt was carefully hidden. "You're right about two of them, but I happen to know I don't have a bottle of wine in the kitchen."

"You do now," he told her, and dropped an arm around her shoulders when they hit the bottom of the stairs. "I picked some up while I was out."

"I do like a man who plans ahead."

"Then you'll love me for the plans I have for later." He took the box from her, walked into the kitchen and set it down on the counter.

She stood in the doorway, her gaze following him as he searched through cupboards for plates and napkins and wineglasses. His hair was shaggy and needed a trim. The jeans he wore now were faded and clung to his butt and legs, displaying what she knew was a well-toned body. He whistled as he opened the bottle of wine and poured each of them a glass of what was probably an outrageously expensive red.

You'll love me for the plans I have for later.

His words echoed in her head, and Georgia tried to shrug them off. Not easy to do, though, when a new and startling discovery was still rattling through her system. Warning bells rang in her mind and a flutter of nerves woke up in the pit of her stomach.

Mouth dry, heart pounding, she looked at Sean and realized what her heart had been telling her for days. Maybe weeks.

She'd done the unthinkable.

She'd fallen in love with Sean Connolly.

Nine

Oh, absolutely not.

She refused to think about it. Simply slammed a wall up against that ridiculous thought and told herself it was jet lag. Or hunger. Probably hunger. Once she got some of that pizza into her, her mind would clear up and she'd be fine again.

"You know, you don't have to do the packing yourself," Sean was saying, and she told herself to pay attention.

"What?"

He snorted a laugh. "Off daydreaming while I'm slaving over a hot pizza box were you?"

"No." God, now she was nervous around him. How stupid was that? He'd seen her naked. She'd made love to the man in every way possible. How could she be nervous over what was, in essence, a blip on the radar?

This wasn't love. This was lust. Attraction. Hell, even *affection.*

But not love.

There, she told herself. Problem solved. *Love* was not a word she was going to be thinking ever again. "What did you say? About the packing?"

"While you take care of putting your house up for sale tomorrow, why don't I make some calls and see about getting movers in here?" He looked around the well-stocked condo kitchen. "You can go through, tell them what you want moved to Ireland and what you're getting rid of, and then stand back and watch burly men do the heavy lifting for you."

Tempting. And expensive. She argued with herself over it for a minute or two, but the truth was, if she did it Sean's way, the whole business could be finished much faster. And wasn't that worth a little extra expense?

Especially if it got her back to Ireland faster? And then hopefully in another week or two, they could end this pretend engagement? She glanced down at the emerald-and-diamond ring on her hand and idly rubbed at the band with her thumb. Soon, it wouldn't be hers anymore. Soon, *Sean* wouldn't be hers anymore.

She lifted her gaze to his and his soft brown eyes were locked on her. Another flutter of something nerve-racking moved in the pit of her stomach, but she pushed it aside. Not love, she reminded herself.

And still, she felt a little off balance. Georgia had to have some time to come to grips with this. To figure out a way to handle it while at the same time protecting herself.

She wasn't an idiot, after all. This hadn't been a part of their deal. It was supposed to be a red-hot affair with no strings attached. A pretend engagement that they would both walk away from when it was over.

And that was just what she would do.

Oh, it was going to hurt, she thought now, as Sean handed her a glass of wine, letting his fingers trail across her skin. When he was out of her life, out of her bed and still in her heart—not that she was admitting he was—it was going to be a pain like she'd never known before.

But she comforted herself with the knowledge that she would be in Ireland, near her sister. She'd have Laura and baby Fiona to help her get over Sean. Shouldn't take more than five or ten years, she told herself with an inner groan.

"So, what do you think?" Sean carried the wine to the table beside the window that overlooked the backyard. "We can have you packed up in a day or two. A lot of your things we can carry back on the jet, what we can't, we'll arrange to ship."

"That's a good idea, Sean." She took a seat, because her knees were still a little weak and it was better to sit down than to fall down. Taking a quick sip of the really great wine, she let it ease the knot in her throat.

Then she picked up the conversation and ran with it. Better to talk about the move. About packers and all of the things she had to do rather than entertain even for a minute that the affection she felt for him could be something else. Losing Sean now was going to hurt. But God help her, if she was really in *love,* the pain would be tremendous.

"There are really only a few things I want to take with me to Ireland," she said. "The rest I'll donate."

That thought appealed to her anyway. She was starting over in Ireland, and the cottage was already furnished, so there was no hurry to buy new things. She could take her time and decide later what she wanted. As for kitchen stuff, it didn't really make sense to ship pots and pans when she could replace them easily enough in Ireland.

All she really wanted from the condo aside from her clothes were family photos, Laura's paintings and a few other odds and ends. What did that say about her, that she'd been living in this condo, surrounded by *stuff* and none of it meant enough to take with her?

She had more of a connection with the cottage than she did with anything here.

"You know," she said, "it's kind of a sad statement that there's so little here I want to take with me. I mean, I was willing to stay here when it clearly didn't mean much to me."

"Why would that be sad?" He sat down opposite her, opened the pizza box and served each of them a slice. "You knew when it was time to move on, is all. Seems to me it's more brave than that. You're moving to a different country, Georgia. Why wouldn't you want to leave the past behind?"

She huffed out a breath and let go of the 'poor me' thoughts that had just begun to form. "How do you do that?"

"What?"

"Manage to say exactly the right thing," she said.

He laughed a little and took a bite of pizza. "Luck, I'd say. And knowing you as I've come to, I thought you might be getting twisted up over all there is to be done and then giving yourself a hard time over it."

Scowling, she told him, "It's a little creepy, knowing you can see into my head so easily."

He picked up his wineglass and toasted her with it. "Didn't say it was easy."

She hoped not, because she *really* didn't want him looking too closely into her mind right now. Twists of emotion tangled inside her and this time she didn't fight them.

Okay, yes. She had feelings for him. Why wouldn't she? He was charming and fun and smart and gorgeous. He was easy to talk to and great in bed, of course she cared about him.

That didn't mean she loved him. Didn't mean anything more than what they had together was important to her.

Even she wasn't buying that one.

Oh, God. No sense in lying to herself, Georgia thought. She'd sew her lips shut and lock herself in a deep dark hole for the rest of her life before she ever admitted the truth to Sean.

This wasn't affection. It wasn't lust. Or hunger.

It was love.

Nothing like the love she had thought she'd found once before.

Now, she couldn't imagine how she had ever convinced herself that she was in love with Mike. Because what she felt for Sean was so much bigger, so much... *brighter,* that it was like comparing an explosion to a sparkler. There simply wasn't a comparison.

This was the kind of love she used to dream of.

And wouldn't you know she'd find it with a man who wouldn't want it? Feelings hadn't been part of their agreement. Love had no place in a secret. A pretense.

So she'd keep her mouth shut and tuck what she felt for him aside until it withered in the dark. It would. Eventually. She hoped.

Oh, God.

She was such an idiot.

"Well," Sean said after a sip of his wine, "I'll admit to you now I've no notion of what you're thinking at this minute. But judging by your expression, it's not making you happy."

Understatement of the century.

"Nothing in particular," she lied smoothly. "Just how much I have to do and how little time I have to do it."

He looked at her for a long minute as if trying to decide to let it lay or not, and finally, thank God, he did.

"So no second thoughts? Being here," he said, glancing around the bright, modern kitchen, "doesn't make you want to rethink your decision?"

She followed his gaze, looking around the room where she'd spent so much alone time in the past year. It was a nice place, she thought, but it had never felt like *hers*. Not like the cottage in Ireland did.

"No," she said, shaking her head slowly. "I came here to live with Laura when my marriage ended and it was what I needed then. But it's not for me now, you know?"

"I do," he said, resting one elbow on the tabletop. "When you find your place, you know it."

"Exactly. What about you? Did you ever want to live somewhere else?"

He grinned. "Leave Dunley?" He shook his head. "I went to college in Dublin and thought it a fine place. I've been all over Europe and to New York several times as well, but none of those bright and busy places tug at me as Dunley does.

"The village is my place, as you said," he told her. "I've no need to leave it to prove anything to myself or anyone else."

"Have you always been so sure of yourself?" She was really curious. He seemed so together. Never doubting himself for a minute. She envied it. At the same time she simply couldn't understand it.

He laughed. "A man who doesn't question himself from time to time's a fool who will soon be slapped down by the fates or whatever gods are paying attention to the jackass of the moment. So of course I question," he said. "I just trust myself to come up with the right answers."

"I used to," she told him and pulled a slice of pepperoni free of the melted cheese and popped it into her mouth. "Then I married Mike and he left me for someone else and I didn't have a clue about it until he was walking out the door." Georgia took a breath and then let it go. "After that, I had plenty of questions, but no faith in my own answers."

"That's changed now, though," he said, his gaze fixed on hers. "You've rebuilt your life, haven't you? And you've done it the way *you* want to. So, I'm thinking your answers were always right, you just weren't ready to hear them."

"Maybe," she admitted. Then, since marriages, both real and pretend, were on her mind, asked, "So, why is it you've never been married?"

He choked on a sip of wine, then caught his breath and said, "There's a question out of the blue."

"Not really. We were talking about my ex—now it's my turn to hear your sad tales. I am your 'fiancée,' after all. Shouldn't I know these things?"

"I suppose you should," he said with a shrug. "Truth is, I was engaged once."

"Really?" A ping of something an awful lot like jealousy sounded inside her. Just went to show her mom was right. She used to tell Georgia, *Never ask a question you don't really want the answer to.*

"Didn't last long." He shrugged again and took a sip of his wine. "Noreen was more interested in my bank account than in me, and she finally decided that she deserved better than a husband who spent most of his time at work."

"Noreen." Harder somehow, knowing the woman's name.

"I let her maneuver me into the thought of marriage," Sean was saying, apparently not clueing in to Georgia's thoughts. "I remember thinking that maybe it was time to be married, and Noreen was there—"

"She was *there?*" Just as *she* had been there, Georgia thought now, when he'd needed a temporary fiancée. Hmm.

He gave her a wry smile. "Aye. I know how it sounds now, but at the time, it seemed easier to let her do what she would than to fight her over it. I was consumed at the time with taking Irish Air to the next level, and I suppose the truth is I didn't care enough to put a stop to Noreen's plans."

Dumbfounded, she just stared at him. "So you would have married her? Not really loving her, you would have married her anyway because it was easier than saying 'no thanks'?"

He shifted uneasily on his chair and frowned a bit at the way she'd put things. "No," he said finally. "I wouldn't have taken that trip down the aisle with her in the end. It wouldn't have worked and I knew it at the time. I was just…"

"Busy?" she asked.

"If you like. Point is," Sean said, "it worked out for the best all around. Noreen left me and married a bank president or some such. And I found you."

Yes, he'd found her. Another temporary fiancée. One he had no intention of escorting down an aisle of any kind. Best to remember that, she told herself.

He lifted his glass and held it out to her, a smile on

his face and warmth in his eyes. Love swam in the pit of her stomach, but Georgia put a lid on it fast. She hadn't planned to love him, and now that she did, she planned to get over it as fast as humanly possible.

So, she'd keep things as they had been between them. Light. Fun. Sexy and affectionate. And when it was over, she'd walk away with her head high, and Sean would never know how she really felt. Georgia tapped her wineglass to his, and when she drank, she thought that the long-gone Noreen had gotten off easy.

Noreen hadn't really loved Sean when she left him, or she'd never have moved on so quickly to someone else.

Georgia on the other hand…it wasn't going to be simple walking away from Sean Connolly.

Georgia was glad they'd come to the wedding. Just seeing the look on Misty's face when she spotted Georgia and Sean had made the trip worthwhile. But it was more than that, too, she told herself. Maybe she'd *had* to attend this wedding. Maybe it was the last step in leaving behind her past so that she could walk straight ahead and never look back.

And dancing with her ex-husband, the groom, was all a part of that. What was interesting was, she felt nothing in Mike's arms. No tingle. No soft sigh of regret for old time's sake. Nothing.

She looked up at him and noticed for the first time that his blue eyes were a little beady. His hair was thinning on top, and she had the feeling that Mike would one day be a comb-over guy. His broad chest had slipped a little, making him a bit thick about the waist, and the whiskey on his breath didn't make the picture any prettier.

Once she had loved him. Or at least thought she had. She'd married him assuming they would be together forever, and yet here she was now, a few years after a divorce she hadn't seen coming and she felt...nothing.

Was that how it would be with Sean one day? Would her feelings for him simply dry up and blow away like autumn leaves in a cold wind?

"You look amazing," Mike said, tightening his arm around her waist.

She did and she knew it. Georgia had gone shopping for the occasion. Her dark red dress had long sleeves, a deep V neckline, and it flared out from the waist into a knee-length skirt that swirled when she moved.

"Thanks," she said, and glanced toward Sean, sitting alone at a table on the far side of the room. Then, willing to be generous, she added, "Misty makes a pretty bride."

"Yeah." But Mike wasn't looking at his new wife. Instead, he was staring at Georgia as if he'd never seen her before.

He executed a fast turn and Georgia had to grab hold of his shoulder to keep from stumbling. He pulled her in even closer in response. When she tried to put a little space between them, she couldn't quite manage it.

"You're engaged, huh?"

"Yes," she said, thumbing the band on her engagement ring. Sean had made quite the impression. Just as she'd hoped, he'd been charming, attentive and, in short, the perfect fiancé. "When we leave here, we're flying home to Ireland."

"Can't believe you're gonna be living in a foreign country," Mike said with a shake of his head. "I don't remember you being the adventurous type at all."

"Adventurous?"

"You know what I mean," he continued, apparently not noticing that Georgia's eyes were narrowed on him thoughtfully. "You were all about fixing up the house.

Making dinner. Working in the yard. Just so—" he shrugged "—boring."

"Excuse me?"

"Come on, Georgia, admit it. You never wanted to try anything new or exciting. All you ever wanted to do was talk about having kids and—" He broke off and sighed. "You're way more interesting now."

Was steam actually erupting from the top of her head? she wondered. Because it really felt like it. Georgia's blood pressure was mounting with every passing second. She had been *boring*? Talking about having kids with your husband was *boring*?

"So, because I was so uninteresting, that's why you slipped out with Misty?" she asked, her voice spiking a little higher than she'd planned. "Are you actually trying to tell me it's *my* fault you cheated on me?"

"Jeez, you always were too defensive," Mike said, and slid his hand down to her behind where he gave her a good squeeze.

Georgia's eyes went wild.

They made a good team.

Sean had been thinking about little else for the past several days. All through the mess of closing up her home and arranging for its sale. Through the packing and the donations to charity and ending the life she'd once lived, they'd worked together.

He was struck by how easy it was, being with her.

Her clever mind kept him on his toes and her luscious body kept him on his knees. A perfect situation, Sean told himself as he sat at the wedding, drinking a beer, considering ways to keep Georgia in his life.

Ever since she'd laid out her ideas to improve the look of his company jets, Sean had been intrigued by possibilities. They got along well. They were a good match. A team, as he'd thought only moments before.

"And damned if I want to lose what we've found," he muttered.

The simplest way, he knew, was to make their engagement reality. To convince her to marry him—not for love, of course, because that was a nebulous thing after all. But because they fit so well. And the more he thought about it, the better it sounded.

Hadn't his cousin Ronan offered very nearly the same deal to his Laura? A marriage based on mutual need and respect. That had worked out, hadn't it? Nodding to himself, he thought it a good plan. The challenge would be in convincing Georgia to agree with him.

But he had time for that, didn't he?

Watching her here, at the wedding of her ex-husband, he was struck again by her courage. Her boldness in facing down those who had hurt her with style and enough attitude to let everyone in the room know that she'd moved on. Happily.

The bride hadn't expected Georgia to show up for the wedding. That had been clear enough when he and Georgia arrived. The stunned shock on the bride's face mingled with the interest from the groom had been proof of that.

Sean frowned to himself and had a sip of the beer sitting in front of him. He didn't much care for the way Georgia's ex-husband took every chance he had to leer at her. But he couldn't blame the man for regretting letting Georgia go in favor of the empty-headed woman he'd now saddled himself with.

Georgia was as a bottle of fine wine while the bride seemed more of a can of flat soda in comparison.

The reception was being held at the clubhouse of a

golf course. Late fall in Ohio was cold, and so the hall was closed up against the night, making the room damn near stifling.

Crepe paper streamers sagged from the corners of the wall where the tape holding them in place was beginning to give. Balloons, as their helium drained away, began to dip and bob aimlessly, as if looking for a way out, and even the flowers in glass vases on every table were beginning to droop.

People who weren't dancing huddled together at tables or crowded what was left of the buffet. Sean was seated near the dance floor, watching Georgia slow dance in the arms of her ex, fighting the urge to go out there and snatch her away from the buffoon. He didn't like the man's hands on her. Didn't like the way Mike bent his head to Georgia and whispered in her ear.

Sean frowned as the music spilled from the speakers overhead and the groom pulled Georgia a bit too tightly against him. Something spiked inside Sean's head and he tightened his grip on the beer bottle so that it wouldn't have surprised him in the least to feel it shatter. Deliberately, he released his hold on the bottle, setting it down carefully on the table.

Then Sean breathed slow and deep, and rubbed the heel of his hand against the center of his chest, unconsciously trying to rub away the hard, cold knot that seemed to have settled there. He gritted his teeth and narrowed his eyes when the groom's hand slipped down to cup Georgia's behind.

Fury swamped his vision and dropped a red haze of anger over his mind. When Georgia struggled to pull free without success, something inside Sean simply snapped. The instinct to protect her roared into life and he went with it. *His* woman, mauled on a dance floor? He bloody well didn't think so.

Sean was halfway out of his chair when Georgia brought the sharp point of one of her high heels down onto the toe of the groom's shoe. While Mike hopped about, whinging about being in pain, Misty ran to her beloved's rescue, and Sean met Georgia halfway between the dance floor and the table.

Her eyes were glinting with outrage, color was high in her cheeks and she'd never been more vividly beautiful to him. She'd saved herself, leaving him nothing to do with the barely repressed anger churning inside him.

His woman, he thought again, and felt the truth of it right down to his bones. And even knowing that, he pulled away mentally from what that might mean. He wouldn't look at it. Not now. Instead, he focused a hard look at the groom and his new bride, then shifted his gaze back to Georgia.

"So then," Sean asked, "ready to leave?"

"Way past ready," Georgia admitted and stalked by him to their table to pick up her wrap and her purse.

He let her go, but was damned if he'd leave this place without making a few things clear to the man he'd like nothing better than to punch into the next week. Misty was clinging to Mike when Sean approached them, but he didn't even glance at the new bride. Instead, his gaze was for the groom, still hobbling unsteadily on one injured foot.

Voice low, eyes hard, Sean said, "I'll not beat a man on his wedding day, so you're safe from me."

Insulted, Mike sputtered, "What the—"

"But," Sean continued, letting the protective instincts rising inside him take over, "you even so much as *think* of Georgia again, I'll know of it. And you and I will have a word."

Misty's mouth flapped open and shut like a baby bird's. Mike flushed dark red, but his eyes showed him for the true coward he was, even before he nodded. Sean left them both standing there, thinking the two of them deserved each other.

When he draped Georgia's wrap about her shoulders, then slid one arm around her waist to escort her from the building, she looked up at him.

"What did you say to him?"

He glanced at her and gave her a quick smile to disguise the fury still pulsing within. "I thanked him for a lovely party and wished him a broken foot."

"I do like your style, Sean," she said, leaning her head against his shoulder.

He kissed the top of her head and took the opportunity to take a long breath of her scent. Then he quipped, "I believe the American thing to say would be, 'back atcha.'"

With the sound of her laughter in his ears, Sean steered her outside to the waiting limousine, and ushered her inside.

With a word to the driver, they were off for the airport so Sean could take his woman home to Ireland.

Ten

A few days later, Sean was standing in Ronan's office in Galway, looking for a little encouragement. Apparently, though, he'd come to the wrong place.

"You're out of your mind," Ronan said.

"Well, don't hold back, cousin," Sean countered, pacing the confines of the office. It was big and plush but at the moment, it felt as if it were the size of a box. There was too much frustrated energy pumping through Sean's brain to let him stand still, and walking in circles was getting him nowhere.

He stopped at the wide window that offered a view of Galway city and the bay beyond. Out over the ocean, layers of dark clouds huddled at the horizon, no doubt bunched up over England but planning their immediate assault on Ireland. Winter was coming in like a mean bitch.

Sean had come into Galway to see Ronan because

his cousin's office was the one place Sean could think
of where they could have a conversation without inter-
ruptions from the seeming *multitude* of women in their
lives. Ronan was, naturally, wrapped up in Laura and
baby Fiona. For Sean, there was his mother, nearly recovered now, and there was Georgia. Beautiful Georgia
who haunted his sleep and infiltrated his every waking
thought.

His woman, he'd thought that night in Ohio, and that
notion had stayed with him. There was something there
between them. He knew it. Felt it. And he'd finally found
a plan to solve his troubles, so he'd needed this time with
Ronan to talk it all out. But for all the help he was finding, he might have stayed home.

"How is it crazy to go after what I want?" he argued
now. "You did it."

Ronan sat back in the chair behind his uncluttered
desk. Tapping the fingers of one hand against that glossy
surface, he stared at Sean with a disbelieving gleam in
his eyes.

"Aye, I did it, just as you're thinking to, so I'm the man
to tell you that you're wrong. You can't ask Georgia to
marry you as a sort of business arrangement."

"Why not?" Sean countered, glancing over his shoulder at his cousin before turning his gaze back to the window and the outside world beyond. "For all your calm
reason now, you did the same with Laura and look how
well that turned out for you."

Ronan scraped one hand across his face. "You idiot.
I almost lost Laura through my own foolishness. She
wouldn't have me, do you not remember that? How I
was forced to chase her down to the airport as she was
leaving me?"

Sean waved that off. The point was, it *had* worked out.

A bump or two in the road, he was expecting. Nothing worthwhile came easy, after all, but in the end, Georgia would agree with him. He'd done a lot of thinking about this, and he knew he was right. Georgia was much more sensible, more reasonable than her sister and he was sure she'd see the common sense in their getting married.

He'd worked it out in his mind so neatly, she had to see it. A businesslike offer of marriage was eminently sensible. With his mother on the mend, the time for ending their faux engagement was fast approaching. And Sean had discovered he didn't want his time with Georgia to be over. He wanted her even more now than he had when this had all begun.

He turned around, leaned one hip against the window jamb and looked at his cousin.

"Georgia's buying a house here," Sean pointed out. "She's opening her business. She won't be running off to California to escape me."

"Doesn't mean she'll greet you with open arms, either," Ronan snapped, then huffed out a breath filled with frustration. "She's already been married to a man who didn't treasure her. Why would she choose another who offers her the same?"

Sean came away from the window in a fast lunge and stood glaring down at Ronan. Damned if he'd be put in the same boat as the miserable bastard who'd caused Georgia nothing but pain. "Don't be comparing me to that appalling excuse of a man who hurt her. I'd not cheat on my wife."

"No, but you won't love her, either," Ronan said, jumping up from his chair to match his cousin glare for glare. "And as she's my sister now, I'll stand for her and tell you myself she *deserves* to be loved, and if you're not the man to do it then bloody well step aside and let her find the one who will."

Those words slapped at Sean's mind and heart, and he didn't much care for it. *Love* wasn't a word Sean was entirely comfortable with. He'd tried to be in love with Noreen and he'd failed. What if he tried with Georgia and failed there, as well? No, he wouldn't risk it. What they had now was good. Strong. Warmth beneath the heat. Caring to go with the passion. Affection that wasn't muddled by trying to label it. Wasn't that enough? Wasn't that more than a lot of people built a life around?

And he'd be damned before he stepped aside for some other man to snatch Georgia in front of his eyes. Which was one of the reasons he'd come up with this plan in the first place. If they ended their engagement—and since Ailish was recovering nicely, that time was coming fast— then he'd be forced to let Georgia go. Watch her find a new man. He'd have to imagine that lucky bastard touching her, kissing her, claiming her in the dark of night— and damned if he'd do *that,* either.

He alone would be the man touching Georgia Page, Sean assured himself, because he could accept no other option. If he did, he'd be over the edge and into insanity in no time at all.

"She had a man who promised her love, as you've just said yourself," Sean argued, jamming both hands into his pockets to hide the fists they'd curled into. Thinking about that man, Georgia's ex, made him want to punch something. That a man such as he had had Georgia and let her go was something Sean would never understand.

"What good did the promise of love do her then?" he asked, more quietly now. "I'm not talking of love but of building a life together."

"Without the first, the second's not much good," Ronan told him with a slow shake of his head.

"Without the first, the second is far less complicated,"

Sean argued. He knew Ronan loved his Laura, and good for him. But love wasn't the only answer. Love was too damn ephemeral. Hard to pin down. If he offered her love, why would she believe him? Why would she trust it when that bastard who had offered the same had crushed her spirit with the word?

No. He could offer Georgia what she wanted. A home. Family. A man to stand at her side and never hurt her as she'd been hurt before. Wasn't that worth something?

"You're a jackass if you really believe that bilge you're shoveling."

"Thanks very much," Sean muttered, then said, "You're missing the point of this, Ronan. If there's no love between us, there's no way for her to be hurt. She'll be safe. I'll see to it."

Ronan skewered him with a look. "You're set on this, aren't you?"

"I am. I've thought this through." In fact, he'd thought of little else since going on that trip to the States with Georgia. He wanted this and so, Sean knew, he could make it happen. He'd never before lost when something mattered as this did. Now wouldn't be the first time. "I know I'm right about this, Ronan."

"Ah, well then." Clapping one hand to Sean's shoulder, Ronan said, "I wish you luck with it, because you're going to need it. And when Georgia coshes you over the head with something heavy, don't be coming to me looking for sympathy."

A tiny speck of doubt floated through the river of Sean's surety, but he paid it no attention at all. Instead, he focused only on his plan, and how to present it to Georgia.

It stormed for a week.

Heavy, black clouds rolled in from the sea, riding an

icy wind that battered the village like a bad-tempered child. The weather kept everyone closed up in their own houses, and Georgia was no different. She'd spent her time hanging pictures and paintings, and putting out the other small things she'd brought with her from California until the cottage was cozy and felt more hers every day.

She missed Sean, though. She hadn't seen him in days. Had spoken to him only briefly on the phone. Laura had told her that Sean and Ronan had spent days and nights all over the countryside, helping the villagers and farmers who were having a hard time through the storm. They'd done everything from mending leaking roofs to ferrying a sick child to the hospital just in time for an emergency appendectomy.

Georgia admired their connection to the village and their determination to see everyone safely through the first big storm of the season. But, God, she'd missed him. And though it pained her, she had finally convinced herself that not seeing him, not having him with her, was probably for the best. Soon, she'd have to get accustomed to his absence, so she might as well start getting used to it.

But it was so much harder than she'd thought it would be. She hadn't planned on that, damn it. She'd wanted the affair with the gorgeous Irishman, and who wouldn't have?

But she hadn't wanted the risk of loving him, and the fact that she did was entirely *his* fault. If he hadn't been so blasted charming and sweet and sexy. If he hadn't been such an amazing lover and so much fun to be around, she never would have fallen. So really, Georgia told herself, none of this was her fault at all.

She'd been hit over the head by the Irish fates and the only way out was pain and suffering. He'd become such a part of her life that cutting him out of it was going to be like losing a limb. Which just irritated her immensely. That she could fall in love when she knew she shouldn't, because of the misery that was now headed her way, was both frustrating and infuriating.

The worst of it now was there was nothing she could do about it. The love was there and she was just going to have to hope that, eventually, it would fade away. In hindsight, she probably shouldn't have accepted Sean's bargain in the first place. But if she hadn't…she would have missed so much.

So she couldn't bring herself to wish away what she'd found with him, even though ending it was going to kill her.

When the sun finally came out, people streamed from their homes and businesses as if they were prisoners suddenly set loose from jail. And Georgia was one of them. She was so eager to get out of her own thoughts, and away from her own company, she raced into town to open her shop and start living the life she was ready to build.

The sidewalks were crowded with mothers who had spent a week trapped with bored children. The tea shop did a booming business as friends and neighbors gathered to tell war stories of storm survival. Shop owners were manning brooms, cleaning up the wreckage left behind and talking to friends as they worked.

Georgia was one of them now. Outside her new design shop, she wielded a broom with the rest of them, and once her place was set to rights, she walked back inside to brew some coffee. She might be in Ireland, but she hadn't yet switched her allegiance from coffee to tea.

The bell over the front door rang in a cheery rattle, and she hurried into the main room only to stop dead when she saw Sean. Everything in her kindled into life. Heat, excitement, want and tenderness tangled together making her nearly breathless. It felt like years since she'd seen him though it had only been a few days. Yes. Irritating.

He looked ragged, tired, and a curl of worry opened up in the center of her chest. The shadow of whiskers on his jaws and the way his hair jutted up, no doubt from him stabbing his fingers through it repeatedly, told her just what a hard few days he'd had. He wore faded jeans, a dark, thickly knit sweater and heavy work boots. And, she thought, he'd never looked more gorgeous.

"How are you?" she asked.

He rubbed one hand across his face, blinked a couple of times, then a half smile curved one corner of his mouth. "Tired. But otherwise, I'll do."

"Laura told me what you and Ronan have been up to. Was it bad?"

"The first big storm of the year is always bad," he said. "But we've got most of the problems in the area taken care of."

"I'm glad. It was scary around here for a day or two," she said, remembering how the wind had howled like the shrieks of the dying. At one point the rain had come down so fiercely, it had spattered into the fire in her hearth.

"I'm sorry I wasn't able to be with you during your first real storm in Dunley," he said, as sunlight outlined him in gold against the window.

"I was fine, Sean. Though I am thinking about getting a dog," she added with a smile. "For the company. Besides, it sounds like you and Ronan had your hands full."

"We did at that." He blew out a breath and tucked his hands into the back pockets of his jeans.

How could a man look *that* sexy in old jeans and beat-up work boots?

"Maeve Carrol's roof finally gave up the ghost and caved in on her."

Georgia started. "Oh, my God. Is she okay?"

"She's well," Sean said, walking farther into the shop, letting his gaze move over the room and all the changes she'd made to it. "Madder than the devil with a drop of holy water in his whiskey, but fine."

She smiled at the image and imagined just how furious Maeve was. The older woman was spectacularly self-sufficient. "So, I'm guessing you and Ronan finally talked her into letting you replace her roof."

"The woman finally had no choice as she's a hole in her roof and lots of water damage." He shook his head. "She nearly floated away on a tide of her own stubbornness. She'll be staying with Ronan and Laura until her cottage is livable again."

Georgia folded her arms across her chest to help her fight the urge to go and wrap her arms around him. "I'm guessing she's not happy about leaving her home."

"You'd think we'd threatened to drag her through the village tied to a rampaging horse." He snorted. "The old woman scared us both half to death. Ronan's been after her for years to let us replace that roof."

"I know. It's nice of you to look out for her."

He glanced at her. "Maeve is family."

"I know that, too," she said and felt that flutter of love inside her again. Honestly, who wouldn't be swooning at the feet of a man like this? Even as that thought circled her brain, Georgia steeled herself. If she wasn't careful, she was going to do something stupid that would alert him to just how much she cared about him.

And that couldn't happen. No way would she live in Dunley knowing that Sean was off at the manor feeling sorry for poor Georgia, who'd been foolish enough to fall in love with him.

"Anyway," she said with forced cheer, "my cottage is sound, thanks to the previous owner. So I was fine."

"Aye," he said softly, brown eyes locked on her face. "You are."

A ripple of sensation slid along her spine at the music in his voice, the heat in his eyes. He was temptation itself, she told herself, and she wondered how she was going to manage living in this town over the years, seeing him and not having him. Hearing the gossip in the village about the women he would be squiring around. And again, she wanted to kick herself for ever agreeing to his crazy proposal.

"You've been working here. Your shop looks good," he said, shifting a quick look around the space. "As do you."

Heat flared inside her, but she refused to acknowledge it. Instead, Georgia looked around her shop, letting her gaze slide over the soft gold walls, the paintings of Laura's that Georgia had hung only that morning.

"Thanks," she said. "The furniture I ordered from the shop in Galway should arrive by end of the week."

She could almost see it, a sleek, feminine desk with matching chair. More chairs for clients, and shelves for what would be her collection of design books. She'd have brightly colored rugs strewn across the polished wood floor and a sense of style that customers would feel the moment they stepped inside.

Georgia was excited about the future even as she felt a pang of regret that Sean wouldn't be a part of it. She took a steadying breath before looking into his soft brown eyes again. And still it wasn't enough. Probably never would be, she thought. He would always hold a piece of her heart, whether he wanted it or not.

Still, she forced a smile. "I think it's really coming along. I'm looking forward to opening the shop for business."

"You'll be brilliant," he said, his gaze level on hers.

"Thanks for that, too." She knew his words weren't empty flattery, and his confidence in her was a blossom of warmth inside her. "And as long as I'm thanking you…we'll add on that I appreciate all your help with the business license."

"We had a deal, didn't we?"

"Yeah," she said, biting at her bottom lip. "We did."

"I spoke to Tim Shannon this morning. He told me that your business license should be arriving by end of the week."

A swirl of nerves fluttered in the pit of her stomach, and she slapped both hands to her abdomen as if to still them.

"Never say you're nervous," he said, smiling.

"Okay, I won't tell you. But I am. A little." She turned her gaze on the front window and stared out at the sunlit street beyond. "This is important to me. I just want to do it right."

"And so you will," Sean said, "and to prove it, I want to hire you."

"What?" That she hadn't expected.

"Do you remember how you reeled off dozens of brilliant ideas on how to improve the interior of my planes?"

"Yes…"

He walked closer, tugged his hands from his pockets and laid them on her shoulders. "I want you to redesign the interiors of all the Irish Air jets."

"You…" She blinked at him.

"Not just the fleet we've got at the moment, either," he told her, giving her shoulders a squeeze. "I want you in on my talks with the plane builders. We can get your input from the beginning that way."

"Redesign your..." It was a wild, exciting idea. And Georgia's mind kicked into high gear despite the shock still numbing parts of her brain.

This was huge. Irish Air as her client would give her an instant name and credibility. It would be an enormous job, she warned herself, expecting nerves or fear to trickle in under the excitement, but they didn't come. All she felt was a rush of expectancy and a thrill that he trusted her enough to turn her loose on the business that meant so much to him.

"I can see the wheels in your mind turning," he said, his mouth curving slightly. "So add this to the mix. You'll have a free hand to make whatever changes you think best. We'll work together, Georgia, and together we'll make Irish Air legendary."

Together. Her heart stirred. Oh, she liked the sound of that, even though more time with Sean would only make the eventual parting that much more painful. How could she *not* love him? He was offering her carte blanche to remake Irish Air because he trusted her.

Shaking her head, she admitted, "I don't even know what to say."

He grinned and she felt a jolt.

"Say yes, of course. I'll be your first client, Georgia, but not your last." He pulled her closer and she looked up into deep brown eyes that shone with pleasure and... something else.

"With Irish Air on your résumé, I guarantee other companies will be beating down your door soon."

"It's great, Sean, really. You won't be sorry for this."

"I've no doubts about that, Georgia," he said, then lifted one hand to smooth her hair back from her face.

At his touch, everything in her trembled, but Georgia fought it. She *had* to fight it, for her own sake.

"There's something else I want to talk to you about." His voice was quiet, thoughtful.

And she knew instinctively what he was going to say. She should have known there would be another reason for his incredible offer. He had come here to tell her their engagement was done. Deal finished. Obviously, he'd offered her that job to take the sting out of the whole thing.

"Let me help," she said, pulling back and away from him. How could she think when his hands were on her? When she was looking into those eyes of his? "Laura told me that Ailish is mostly recovered now and I'm really glad."

"Thank you," he said, "and yes, she is. She'll see her doctor this week, then all will be back to normal."

Normal. Back to life without Sean.

"So she'll be headed back to Dublin?"

"No," Sean said. "Mother's decided she wants to come home to Dunley. I offered her the left wing of the manor, but she says she's no interest in living with her son." He shrugged and laughed a little. "So she's opted for moving into the gatehouse on the estate."

"The gatehouse?" Georgia didn't remember ever noticing a gatehouse at Sean's place.

"It's what we call it, anyway," he said with a smile. "It was originally built for my grandmother to live in when she moved out of the manor in favor of my parents. Mother's always loved it, and there's plenty of room there for her friends to visit."

"Oh, okay. Well, it's nice that she'll be closer. I really like your mother."

"I know you do," Sean said. "But the thing is, with mother recovering, it's time we talked about our bargain."

"It's okay." Georgia cut him off. She didn't want him to say the words. "You don't have to say it. Ailish is well, so we're finished with this charade."

She tugged at the ring on her finger, but he reached out and stilled her hand. Georgia looked up at him.

"I don't want to be done with it," he blurted, and hope shot through her like sunlight after the storm they'd just lived through.

She swallowed hard and asked, "What?"

"I want us to marry," he said, curling her fingers into her palm to prevent her from taking off the ring.

"You do?" Love dazzled her. She looked into his eyes and saw them shine. She felt everything in her world setting itself straight again. In one split instant, she saw their lives spiraling out into a wonderful future. The home they'd make. The children. The family. She saw love and happiness and everything she'd ever wished for.

The sad cynic inside her died, and Georgia was glad to see her go.

And then he continued talking.

"It makes sense," he told her, a gorgeous smile on his face. "The village is counting on it. My mother's got the thing half-planned already. We work well together. You must admit we make a hell of a good team. We're great in bed together. I think we should simply carry on with the engagement and go through with the marriage. No one ever has to know we didn't marry for love."

Eleven

There, Sean told himself. He'd done it. Laid out his plan for her, and now she'd see exactly what they could have together. Looking into her eyes, he saw them alight, then watched worriedly as that light dimmed. He spoke up fast, hoping to see her eyes shine again.

"There's no sense in us breaking up when any fool could see we've done well together," he said, words rushing from him as her eyes went cool and a distance seemed to leap up between them.

He moved in closer and told himself she hadn't actually moved *away,* just to one side. "You're a sensible woman, Georgia. Clear-thinking. I admire that about you, along with so many other facets of you."

"Well, how nice for you that I'm such a calm person."

"I thought so." He frowned. "But somehow, I've insulted you."

"Oh, why would I be insulted by *that?*"

"I've no idea," he said, but watched her warily. "I realize I've caught you off guard with this, but you'll see, Georgia. If you'll but take a moment to think it through, you'll agree that this is the best way for both of us."

"You've decided that, have you?" She snapped a look at him that had the hackles at the back of his neck standing straight up.

This wasn't going as he'd thought it would, yet he had no choice but to march on, to lay everything out for her.

"I did. I've done considerable thinking about the two of us since we took that trip to California."

"Have you?"

Her tone was sweet, calm, and he began to relax again. This was the Georgia he knew so well. A temper, aye. What's life without a little seasoning after all, but a reasonable woman at the heart of it.

"I'm saying we work well together and there's no reason for us to separate." When her gaze narrowed, he hurried on. "The entire village is expecting a wedding. If we end things now, there'll be questions and whispers and gossip that will last for years."

"That's not what you said when we started this," she countered. *"Oh, they'll all think you've come to your senses,"* she added in such a true mimic of his own voice and words she had him flinching.

"It's different now," he insisted.

"How? How is it different?"

He rubbed one hand over his face, fatigue clawing at him even as his muddled mind fought for survival. "You're a part of things in Dunley, as am I. They'll wonder. They'll talk."

"Let them," she snapped. "Isn't that what a *sensible* woman would say?"

"Clearly that word upsets you, though I've no idea

why. You're a lovely woman, Georgia, with a sound mind and a clear vision." He pushed on, determined to make her see things his way, though the ground beneath his feet felt suddenly unstable. "You're rational, able to look at a situation and see it for what it is. Which is why I know you'll agree with me on this. Ronan insisted you wouldn't, of course, but he doesn't know you as I do…"

"Ronan?" she asked, turning her head and glancing at him from the corner of her eye. "You discussed this with Ronan?"

"Why wouldn't I?" He stiffened. "He's as close as a brother to me, and I wanted to get it all set in my mind before I came to you with it."

"And now you have?"

"I do," Sean told her, and felt worry begin to slither through him. She wasn't reacting as he'd expected. He'd thought that his sensible Georgia would smile up at him and say, *Good idea, Sean. Let's do it.* Instead, the distance between them seemed to be growing despite the fact she was standing right in front of him.

She looked down at the emerald-and-diamond ring on her finger, and when he caught her hand in his, he felt better. She was considering his proposal, then, though he'd have expected a bit more excitement and a little less biting his damned head off.

"If you'll just take a moment to consider it, I know you'll agree. You're not a woman to muddy your thinking by looking through the wavery glass of emotion."

"Oh, no," she whispered, rubbing her thumb against the gold band of her ring. "I'm cool and calm. That's me. No emotions. Little robot Georgia."

"Robot?" He frowned at her. "What're you talking about?"

"Logical," she repeated. "Rational. If I come when you whistle I could be your dog."

He scrubbed the back of his neck. Maybe he shouldn't have come here first thing this morning. Maybe he should have waited. Gotten some damn sleep before talking to her. For now, he felt as though even his own thoughts were churning. He couldn't lay a finger on how he'd gone wrong here, but he knew he had.

The only way out was to keep talking, hoping he'd stumble on the words he needed so desperately. And why was it, he thought wildly, that when he most needed the words, they'd dried up on him?

"Not a robot now, but a dog?" Sean shook his head. "You've got this all wrong, Georgia. 'Tis my fault you're not understanding me," he said benevolently. "I've not made myself clear enough."

"Oh," she told him with a choked-off laugh, "you're coming through loud and clear."

"I can't be, no, or you wouldn't be standing there spitting fire at me with your eyes."

"Really?" She cocked her head to one side and studied him. "How should I react to this oh-so-generous proposal?"

Temper slapped him. He was offering marriage here, not a year in a dungeon. For all the way she was acting, you wouldn't believe he was trying to make her his wife but instead ordering her to swim her way back to America.

"A kiss wouldn't be out of hand, if you're asking me. It's not every day I ask a woman to marry me, you know."

"And so graciously, too." She fiddled with her ring again, thumb sliding across the big green stone. "I should probably apologize."

"No need for that," he said, worry easing back an inch or so now. "I've caught you by surprise, is all."

"Oh, you could say that." She pulled her hand free of his. "And your proposal to Noreen, was it every bit this romantic?"

"Romantic? What's romance to do with this?"

"Nothing, obviously," she muttered.

"And I never proposed to Noreen," he told her hotly. "That just…happened."

"Poor you," Georgia told him with sarcasm dripping off each word. "How you must have been taken advantage of."

"I didn't say that—" He shook his head and blew out a breath. "I've no idea what I'm saying now, you've got me running in circles so."

"Not sensible enough for you?"

"Not by half, no," he said flatly. "You're behaving oddly, Georgia, if you don't mind my saying." Reaching for her, he blinked when she batted his hands away. "What was that for?"

"Oh, let me count the reasons," she muttered, stalking away from him to pace back and forth across the narrow width of the shop.

The short heels of her boots clacked loudly against the wood floor and sounded to Sean like a thundering heartbeat.

"You want me to marry you because your mother's making plans and the *village* will be disappointed."

"That's only part of it," he argued, feeling control slipping away from him somehow.

"Yes, of course." She snapped him a furious glance. "There's how well we work together, too."

"There is."

"And we're such a good team, right?" Her eyes flashed. "And let's not forget how good we are in bed together."

"It's a consideration, I think you'll agree, when wanting to marry." His tone was as stiff as his spine as he faced the rising fury in her eyes.

"Sure, wouldn't want to waste your time on a sensible, rational, logical woman who sucked in bed."

"A harsh way of putting it—"

She held up one hand to keep him from saying anything else, and he was shocked enough to obey the silent command.

"So basically, you don't want anything as pesky as *love* involved in this at all."

"Who said anything about love?" he demanded, as something cold and hard settled in the center of his chest.

"Exactly my point."

Swallowing his rising anger, he kept his voice calm as he pointed out, "You're not talking sense, Georgia."

"Wow, I'm not?" She flashed him a look out of eyes that had gone as dark as the ocean at night. "How disappointing for you."

Watery winter sunlight slanted into the room through the front windows and seemed to lay across Georgia like a blessing. Her hair shone, her features were golden and the flash in her eyes was unmistakable.

Still, Sean had come here to claim her and he wasn't willing to give up on that. "You're taking this the wrong way entirely, Georgia. You care for me, and I for you—"

"Care for?" she repeated, her voice hitching higher. "Care for? I *love* you, you boob."

Sean was staggered, and for the first time in his life, speechless.

"Hah!" She stabbed one finger in the air, pointing it at him like a blade. "I see you hadn't considered *that* in all of your planning. Why would rational, logical, *sensible* Georgia be in love?"

She loved him? Heat blistered his insides even as words tangled on his tongue.

"Well, I can't explain that. It's really not sensible at all," Georgia muttered, pushing both hands through her hair before dropping her hands to her sides and glaring at him. "At the moment, it feels downright stupid."

"It's not stupid," Sean blurted out, crossing to her and taking hold of her shoulders before she could dodge his touch again. Love? She loved him? This was perfect. "It's more reason than ever for you to marry me. You love me, Georgia. Who the bloody hell else would you marry?"

"Nobody." She yanked free of his grip.

"That makes no sense at all."

"Then you're not paying attention," she snapped. "You think I want to marry a man who doesn't love me? *Again?* No, thanks. I've already had that and am in no way interested in doing it all over."

"I'm nothing like that inexcusable shite you married and you bloody well know it," he argued, feeling the need to defend himself.

"Maybe not, but what you're offering me is a fake marriage."

"It would be real."

"It would be legal," she argued. "Not real."

"What the bloody hell's the difference?"

"If you don't *know* what the difference is," she countered, "then there's no way to explain it to you." She took a long breath and said, "I've come to Ireland to build myself a life. *Myself.* And just because I made the mistake of falling in love with you doesn't mean I'm willing to throw those plans away."

"Who's asking you to?" he demanded, wondering if

she loved him as she claimed, how she could be so stubbornly blind to what they shared. What they *could* share.

"I'm done with you, Sean. It's over. No engagement. No marriage. No nothing." She grabbed his arm and tugged him toward the door.

Sunlight washed the street and, for the first time, Sean noted that a few of the villagers had gathered outside the door. Drawn, no doubt by the rising voices. Nothing an Irishman liked better than a good fight—either participating or witnessing.

"Now get out and go away."

"You're throwing me out of your shop?" He dug in his heels and she couldn't budge him another inch.

"Seems the 'sensible' thing to do," she countered, her gaze simply boiling with temper.

"There's nothing sensible about you at the moment, I'm sorry to say."

"Thank you! I don't feel sensible. In fact, I may never be sensible again." She tapped the tip of her index finger against the center of his chest. "In fact, I feel *great*. It's liberating to say exactly what you're thinking and feeling.

"I've always done the right thing—okay, the sensible thing. But no more. And if you don't want me to redesign Irish Air, that's fine with me." She shook her hair back from her face. "I hear Jefferson King lives somewhere around here—I'll go see *him* about a job if I have to."

"Jefferson King?" The American billionaire who now lived on a sheep farm near Craic? Just the thought of Georgia working in close quarters with another man gave Sean a hard knot in the pit of his belly. Even if that man was married and a father.

Georgia belonged here. With him. Nowhere else.

"There's no need for that," he said sharply. "I don't

break my word. I've hired you to do the job and I'll expect you to do it well."

Surprise flickered briefly in her eyes. At least he had that satisfaction. It didn't last long.

"Good." Georgia gave him a sharp nod. "Then we're agreed. Business. *No* pleasure."

Outside the shop, muttering and conversations rose along with the size of the crowd. All of Dunley would be out there soon, Sean thought, gritting his teeth. Damned if he'd give the village more grist to chew on. If she wouldn't see reason, then he'd leave her now and try again another day to batter his way through that hard head of hers.

He lowered his voice and said, "You've a head like stone, Georgia Page."

"And so is your heart, Sean Connolly," she told him furiously.

Someone outside gasped and someone else laughed.

"This is the way you talk to a man who offers you marriage?" he ground out.

"A man who offered me *nothing*. Nothing of himself. Nothing that matters."

"Nothing? I offer you my name and that's nothing?" His fury spiked as he stared down into those blue eyes flashing fire at him.

She didn't back down an inch and even while furious he could admire that, as well.

"Your name, yes," Georgia said. "But that's all. You don't offer your heart, do you, Sean? I don't think you'd know how."

"Is that right?" Her words slapped at him and a part of him agreed with her. He'd never once in his life risked love. Risked being out of control in that way. "Well, I don't remember hearts being a part of our bargain, do you?"

"No, but with *people,* sometimes hearts get in the way."

"Oooh," someone said from outside, "that was a good one."

"Hush," another voice urged, "we'll miss something."

Sean dragged in a breath and blew it out again, firing a furious glare at their audience then looking back again to Georgia. "I'll be on my way, then, since we've nothing more to talk about."

"Good idea." She folded her arms over her chest and tapped the toe of her shoe against the floor in a rapid staccato that sounded like machine gun fire.

"Fine, then." He turned, stepped outside and pushed his way through the small crowd until he was out on the street. All he wanted now was to walk off this mad and think things through. He stopped when Georgia called his name and turned to her, hoping—foolishly—that she'd changed her mind.

She whipped her right arm back and threw her engagement ring at him. It hit Sean dead in the forehead and pain erupted as she shouted, "No engagement. No marriage!"

She slammed the door to punctuate her less than sensible shout.

Sean heard someone say, "She's a good arm on her for all she's small."

Muttering beneath his breath, Sean bent down to pick up the ring and when he straightened, Tim Casey asked, "So, the wedding'll be delayed, then? If you can keep her angry at you until January, I'll win the pool."

Sean glanced at the closed door of the shop and imagined the furious woman inside. "Shouldn't be a problem, Tim."

* * *

An hour later, Ailish was sitting in Laura's front parlor, a twist of disgust on her lips. "Well, it's happened."

"What?" Laura served the older woman a cup of tea, then took one for herself before sitting down on the couch beside her. "What happened?"

"Just what we've been waiting for," Ailish told her. "I heard from Katie, Sean's housekeeper, that Mary Donohue told her that not an hour ago, your sister threw her engagement ring at Sean. I'd say that ends the 'bargain' you told me about."

Laura groaned. Since the phone call with Ailish, when the sly woman had gotten Laura to confess all about Sean's and Georgia's ridiculous "deal," the two of them had been co-conspirators. Sean's mother was determined to see him married to a "nice" woman and to start giving her grandchildren. Laura was just as determined to see her sister happy and in love. And from what Laura had noted lately, Georgia *was* in love. With Sean. So, if she could...help, she would.

But, this new wrinkle in the situation did not bode well.

Ailish had been convinced that if they simply treated the wedding as a fait accompli, then Sean and Georgia would fall into line. Laura, knowing her sister way better, hadn't bought it for a minute, but she hadn't been able to think of anything else, either. So Ailish had ordered a cake, Laura had reserved canvas tenting for the reception and had already made a few calls to caterers in Galway and Westport.

Not that they would need any of that, now.

"Then it's over," Laura said. "I was really hoping they might actually realize that they belonged together and that it would all work out."

"They *do* belong together," Ailish said firmly, pausing to take a sip of her tea. "We're not wrong about that."

"It doesn't really matter what we think though, does it?" Laura shook her head. "Damn it, I knew Georgia was going to end up hurt."

Ailish gave a delicate, ladylike snort. "From what I heard, I'd say Sean was the one hurt. That was a very big emerald, and apparently she hit him square in the middle of his forehead." Nodding, she added, "Perhaps it knocked some sense into the man."

"Doubt it," Laura grumbled, then added, "no offense."

"None taken." Ailish reached out and patted her hand. "I've never seen my son so taken with a woman as he is with our Georgia, and by heaven, if he's too stubborn to see it, then we'll just have to help the situation along."

"What've you got in mind?" Laura watched the older woman warily.

"A few ideas is all," Ailish said, "but we may need a little help…"

At that moment, Ronan walked into the room, cradling his baby daughter in his arms. He took one look at the two women with their heads together and made a quick about-face, trying for a stealthy escape.

"Not one more step, Ronan Connolly," Ailish called out.

He stopped, turned back and looked at each woman in turn. Narrowing his eyes on them, he said, "You're plotting something, aren't you?"

"*Plotting*'s a harsh word," Laura insisted.

He frowned at her.

"None of your glowering now, Ronan," his aunt told him. "This is serious business here."

"I'll not have a part in a scheme against Sean," he warned.

"'Tis *for* Sean," Ailish corrected him. "Not against him. I am his mother, after all."

"Oh, aye, that makes a difference."

Ailish turned a hard look on her nephew and Laura hid a smile.

"We'll be needing your help, and I want no trouble from you on this," Ailish said.

"Oh, now, I think I'd best be off and out of this—"

"Give it up, Ronan," Laura told him with a slow shake of her head. "You're lost against her and you know it." Turning to the older woman, she said with admiration, "You'd have been a great general."

"Isn't that a lovely thing to say?" Ailish beamed at her and then waved Ronan closer. "Come now, it won't be a bit of trouble to you. You'll see."

Ronan glumly walked forward, but bent his head to his daughter and whispered, "When you're grown, you're not allowed to play with your aunt Ailish."

Twelve

"Damn it Georgia, I knew this was going to happen!" Laura dropped onto the sofa and glared at her sister.

"Well, congrats, you must be psychic!" Georgia curled her legs up under her and muttered, "Better than being sensible, anyway."

"So now what?" Laura reached over and turned up the volume on the baby monitor she'd set on the nearby table. Instantly, the soft sound of Beethoven slipped into the room along with the sighs of a sleeping baby.

Georgia listened to the sounds and felt a jab of something sweet and sharp around her heart. If she hadn't loved Sean, she might have gotten married again someday. But now she was stuck. She couldn't marry the one she loved and wouldn't marry anyone else. Which left her playing the part of favorite auntie to Laura and Ronan's kids.

"Now nothing," Georgia told her and couldn't quite stop a sigh. "It's over and that's the end of it."

"Doesn't make sense," Laura muttered. "I've *seen* the way Sean looks at you."

"If I *pay* you, will you let this go?" Georgia asked.

"I don't know why you're mad at me. You should be fighting with Sean."

"I did already."

"Sounds like you should again."

"To what point?" Georgia shook her head. "We said what we had to say and now we're done."

"Yeah," Laura told her wryly. "I can see that."

"I'll get over it and *him*," Georgia added, remembering Sean's insulting proposal and the look of shock on his face when she told him *thanks, but no, thanks*. Idiot. She dropped her head onto the back of the couch. "Maybe it's like a bad case of the flu. I'll feel like I'm going to die for a few days and then I'll recover." Probably.

"Oh, that's good."

Georgia lifted her head and speared her sister with a dark look. "You could indulge my delusions."

"I'd rather encourage you to go fight for what you want."

"So I can go and beg a man to love me?" Georgia stiffened. "No, thank you. I'll pass on that, thanks."

"I didn't say *beg*. I said *fight*."

"Just leave it alone, okay? Enough already."

She didn't want to keep reliving it all. As it was, her own mind kept turning on her, replaying the scene over and over again. *Why* did she have to tell him she loved him?

Scowling, Laura looked across the room at her husband. "This is your fault."

"And what did I do?"

"Sean's your cousin. You should beat him up or something."

Before Ronan could respond to that, Georgia laughed. "Thanks for the thought, but I don't want him broken and bleeding."

"How about bruised?" Laura asked. "I could settle for bruised."

"No," she said. She was bruised enough for both of them, and she couldn't even blame Sean for it. She was the one who'd fallen in love when she shouldn't have. She was the one who had built up unrealistic dreams and then held them out all nice and shiny for him to splinter. And even now, she loved him. So who was the real idiot? "It's done. It's over. Let's move on."

"Always said you were the sensible one," Ronan piped up from across the room, and then he shivered when Georgia sent him a hard look.

"God, I hate that word."

"I'll make a note of it," Ronan assured her.

"Oh, relax, Ronan," Georgia told him. "I'm not mad at you. I'm mad at *me*."

"For what?" Laura demanded.

"I never should have told him I loved him."

"Why shouldn't you?" her sister argued. "He should know exactly what he's missing out on."

"Yeah," Georgia said, pushing up from the couch, unable to sit still. "I'm sure it's making him crazy, losing me."

"Well, it should!" Laura shot a dark look at her husband and Ronan lifted both hands as if to say, *I had nothing to do with this.*

"Excuse me, Miss Laura."

Patsy Brennan, the housekeeper, walked into the front room. "But Mickey Culhane is here to see Miss Georgia."

Georgia looked to Ronan. "Who's Mickey Culhane?"

"He owns a farm on the other side of Dunley. It was his son Sean drove to hospital during the storm." To Patsy, he added, "Show him in."

"Why would he want to see me?" Georgia wondered.

"How would I know?" Laura asked unconvincingly.

Georgia looked at her sister wish suspicion, then turned to face the man walking into the front parlor.

Mickey was about forty, tall, with thick red hair and weathered cheeks. He nodded to Ronan and Laura, then turned his gaze to Georgia. "I've heard about the troubles you and Sean are having, Miss, and wanted to say that you shouldn't be too hard on him. He's a fine man. Drove thirty kilometers into the teeth of that storm to get my boy to safety."

Georgia felt a flush of heat fill her cheeks. "I know he did, and I'm glad your son's okay."

"He is, yes." Mickey grinned. "Thanks to Sean. Without that Rover of his, we'd never have gotten the boy to help in time. You should probably think more kindly of him, is all I'm saying." He looked to Ronan and nodded. "Well, I've to be off and home for supper."

"G'night, Mickey," Ronan called as the man left.

"What was that all about?" Georgia asked the room in general as she stared after the farmer thoughtfully.

For three days, Sean stayed away from Dunley, from the cottage, giving himself time to settle and giving Georgia time to miss him. And by damn, he thought, she'd better well miss him as he missed her.

During those three days, he threw himself into work. For him, there was no other answer. When his mind was troubled or there was a problem he was trying to solve, work was always the solution.

He had meetings with his engineers, with HR, with contracts and publicity. He worked with pilots and asked for their input on the new planes and tried not to focus on the woman who would be designing their interiors.

He went in to the office early and stayed late. Anything to avoid going home. To Dunley. To the manor. Where the emptiness surrounding him was suffocating. And for three days, despite his best efforts, his mind taunted him with thoughts of Georgia. With the memory of her face as she said *I love you, you boob.*

Had ever a man been both insulted and given such a gift at the same time?

Pushing away from his desk, he walked to the window and stared out over Galway. The city lights shone in the darkness and over the bay, moonlight played on the surface of the water. The world was the same as it had been before Georgia, he thought. And yet…

A cold dark place inside him ached in time with the beat of his heart. He caught his own reflection in the window glass and frowned at the man looking back at him. He knew a fool when he saw one.

Sean Connolly didn't quit. He didn't give up on what he wanted just because he'd hit a hitch in his plans. If he had, Irish Air would be nothing more than a dream rather than being the top private airline in the world.

So a beautiful, strong-willed, infuriating woman wasn't going to stop him either.

But Georgia wasn't his problem and he knew it. The fact was, he'd enjoyed hearing her say she loved him. Had enjoyed knowing that she had said those three words, so fraught with tension and risk, first. It put him more in control, as he'd always preferred being. He hadn't allowed himself to take that step into the unknown. To risk his pride. And yet, he told himself, if there was no risk, there was no reward. He hadn't stepped away from the dare and risk of beginning his airline, had he?

"No, I did not," he told the man in the glass.

Yet, when it had come to laying his heart at the feet of a woman who had looked furious enough to kick it back in his face…he'd balked. Did that make him a coward or a fool?

He knew well that *fool* would be the word Ronan would choose. And his mother. And no doubt Georgia had several apt names for him about now.

But to Sean's way of thinking, what this was, was a matter of control. He would be in charge. He would keep their battle on his turf, so to speak—and since she had up and moved to Ireland she'd helped him in that regard already. What he had to do now was get her to confess her feelings again and then allow that perhaps he might feel the same.

"Perhaps," he sneered. What was the point in lying to himself, he wondered. Of course he loved her. Maybe he always had. Though he hadn't meant to. That certainly hadn't been part of his plan. But there Georgia Page was, with her temper, her wit, her mind. There wasn't a thing about her that didn't tear at him and fire him up all at once. She was the woman for him. Now he'd just to make her see the truth of it.

"And how will you do that when she's no doubt not speaking to you?"

He caught the eye of the man in the glass again and he didn't like what he saw. A man alone. In the dark, with the light beyond, out of reach.

Until and unless he found a way to get Georgia back in his life, he knew the darkness would only grow deeper until it finally swallowed him.

On that thought, he managed a grin as an idea was born. Swiftly, he turned for his desk, grabbed up the phone and made a call.

For the past few days, Georgia had been besieged.

Mickey Culhane had been the first but certainly not the last. Every man, woman and child in Dunley had an opinion on the situation between she and Sean and lined up to share it.

Children brought her flowers and told her how Sean always took the time to play with them. Men stopped in to tell her what a fine man Sean was. He never reneged on a bet and was always willing to help a friend in trouble. Older women regaled her with stories of Sean's childhood. Younger women told of how handsome and charming he was—as if she needed to be convinced of *that*.

In essence, Dunley was circling the wagons, but rather than shutting Georgia out for having turned on one of their own, they were deliberately trying to drag her into the heart of them. To make her see reason and "forgive Sean for whatever little thing he might have done."

The only thing she really had to forgive him for was *not* loving her. Well, okay, that and his terrible proposal. But she wouldn't have accepted a proposal from him even if he'd had violins playing and rose petals at her feet— not if he didn't love her.

But in three days, she hadn't caught even so much as a glimpse of him. Which made her wonder where he was even while telling herself it was none of her business where he was or *who* he was with. That was a lie she couldn't swallow. It ate her up inside wondering if Sean had already moved on. Was he with some gorgeous Irish redhead, already having put the Yank out of his mind?

That was a lowering thought. She was aching for him,

and the bastard had already found someone else? Was she that forgettable, really?

The furniture deliverymen had only just left when the bell over the front door sang out in welcome. Georgia hurried into the main room from the kitchen and stopped dead in her tracks.

"Ailish."

Sean's mother looked beautiful, and even better, *healthy*. She wore black slacks and a rose-colored blouse covered by a black jacket. A small clutch bag was fisted in her right hand.

"Good morning," she said, a wide smile on her face.

Georgia's stomach dropped. First, it was the villagers who'd come to support Sean and now his mother. Georgia seriously didn't know how much more she could take.

"Ailish," she said, "I really like you, but if you've come to tell me all about how wonderful your son is, I'd rather not hear it."

One eyebrow winged up and a smile touched her mouth briefly. "Well, if you already know his good points, we could talk about his flaws."

Georgia laughed shortly. "How much time do you have?"

"Oh, Georgia, I do enjoy you." Ailish chuckled, stepped into the shop and glanced around the room. "Isn't this lovely? Clearly feminine, yet with a strong, clear style that can appeal to a man, as well."

"Thank you." It was the one thing that had gone well this week, Georgia thought. Her furniture was in and she had her shop arranged just as she wanted. Now all she needed were clients. Well, beyond Irish Air. She'd talked to Sean's secretary just the day before and set up an appointment to go into Galway to meet with him.

She was already nervous. She hated that.

"You're in love with him."

"What?" Georgia jolted out of her thoughts to stare at Ailish, making herself comfortable on one of the tufted, blue chairs.

"I said, you're in love with my son."

Awkward. "Well, don't hold that against me. I'm sure I'll get over it."

Ailish only smiled. "Now why would you want to do that?"

Georgia sighed. The woman was Sean's *mother*. How was she supposed to tell the poor woman that her son was a moron? A gorgeous, sexy, funny moron? There was just no polite way to do it, so Georgia only said, "There's no future in it for me, Ailish. Sean's a nice guy—" surely she was scoring Brownie points with the universe here "—but we—I—it just didn't work out."

"Yet." Ailish inspected her impeccable manicure, then folded her hands on her lap. "I've a great fondness for you, Georgia, and I'm sure my son does, as well."

God. Could she just bash her own head against a wall until she passed out? That would be more pleasant than this conversation. "Thank you. I like you, too, really. But Ailish, Sean doesn't love me. There is no happy ending here."

"But if there were, you'd take it?"

Her heart twisted painfully in her chest. A happy ending? Sure, she'd love one. Maybe she should go out into the faery wood and make a wish on the full moon, as Sean had told her.

"Well?" the woman urged. "If my son loved you, then would you have him?"

Oh, she would have him so fast, his head would spin. She would wrap herself around him and let herself drown in the glory of being loved, really loved, by the only man she wanted. Which was about as likely to happen as stumbling across calorie-free chocolate.

"He doesn't, so the question is pointless."

"But I notice you didn't answer it."

"Ailish…" Such a nice woman. Georgia just didn't have the heart to tell her that it had all been a game. A stupid, ridiculous game cooked up by a worried son.

"You've a kind heart, Georgia." Ailish rose, walked to her and gave her a brief, hard hug. Emotion clogged Georgia's throat. She really could have used a hug from her own mother, so Ailish was filling a raw need at the moment. She would have loved this woman as a mother-in-law.

Ailish pulled back then and patted Georgia's cheek. "As I said, you've a kind heart. And a strong spirit. Strong enough, I think, to shake Sean's world up in all the right ways."

Georgia opened her mouth to speak, but Ailish cut her off.

"Don't say anything else, dear. Once spoken, some words are harder to swallow than others." She tucked her purse beneath her arm, touched one hand to her perfect hair and then headed for the door. "I'm glad I came today."

"Me, too," Georgia said. And she was. In spite of everything, these few minutes with Sean's mother had eased a few of the ragged edges inside her heart.

"I'll see you tonight at dinner, dear." Ailish left and the bell over Georgia's door tinkled into the sudden stillness.

It was cold, and the wind blowing in from the ocean was damp. But Laura's house was warm and bright, with a fire burning in the hearth and Beast and Deidre curled up together in front of it. The two dogs were inseparable,

Georgia mused, watching as Beast lay his ugly muzzle down on top of Deidre's head.

Now here was an example of a romance between the Irish and a Yank that had turned out well. So well that, together, the two dogs had made puppies that would be born sometime around Christmas.

Stooping to stroke Beast's head and scratch behind his ears, Georgia told herself that she would adopt one of the pups and she'd have her own Beast junior. She wouldn't be alone then. And she could pour all the love she had stored up to give on a puppy that would love her back.

"Thanks for that," she murmured, and Beast turned his head just far enough to lick her hand.

"Georgia," Laura called, and peeked into the room from the hallway. "Would you do me a favor and go to the wine cellar? Ronan forgot to bring up the red he's picked out for dinner, and I'd like it open and breathing before Ailish gets here."

"Sure," she answered, straightening up. "Where is it?"

"Oh. Um," Laura worried her bottom lip. "He, um, said he set it out, so you should find it easily enough."

"Motherhood's making you a little odd, honey," Georgia said with a smile.

Laura grinned. "Worth every burnt-out brain cell."

"I bet." Georgia was still smiling as she walked down the hall and made the turn to the stairs.

This family dinner idea of Laura's was good, she told herself. Nice to get out of her house. To get away from Dunley and all the well-meaning villagers who continued to sing Sean's praises.

As she opened the heavy oak door and stepped into the dimly lit wine cellar, she thought she heard something behind her. Georgia turned and looked up at Ronan as he stepped out of the shadows. "Ronan?"

He gave her an apologetic look then closed the door.

"Hey!" she called, "Ronan, what're you doing?"

On the other side, the key turned in the lock and she grabbed the doorknob, twisting it uselessly. If this was a joke, it was a bad one. Slapping her hand against the door, she shouted, "Ronan, what's going on here?"

"'Tis for your own good, Georgia," he called back, voice muffled.

"*What* is?"

"I am," Sean said from behind her.

She whirled around so fast, she nearly lost her balance. Sean reached out to steady her but she jumped away from his touch as if he were a leper. He buried the jolt of anger that leaped to the base of his throat and stuffed his hands into his pockets, to keep from reaching for her again only to be rebuffed.

"What're you doing here?" Georgia demanded.

"Waiting for you," he said tightly. Hell, he'd been in the blasted wine cellar for more than an hour, awaiting her arrival for the family dinner he'd had Laura arrange.

The cellar was cool, with what looked like miles of wooden racks filled with every kind of wine you could imagine. Pale lights overhead spilled down on them, creating shadows and the air was scented by the wood, by the wine and, Sean thought…by *her*.

Having Ronan lock her inside with him had been his only choice. Otherwise the stubborn woman would have escaped him and they'd *never* say the things that had to be said.

"I've been waiting awhile for you. Opened a bottle of wine. Would you like some?"

She folded her arms across her middle, pulling at the fabric of her shirt, defining the curve of her breasts in a way that made his mouth water for her. With supreme effort he turned from the view and poured her a glass without waiting for her answer.

He handed it to her and she drank down half of it as if it were medicine instead of a lovely pinot.

"What do you want, Sean?" she said, voice tight, features closed to him.

"Five bloody minutes of your time, if it's all the same to you," he answered, then took a sip of his own wine, telling himself that *he* was supposed to be the cool head here.

But looking at her as she stood in front of him, it took everything in him to stand his ground and not grab her up and kiss her until she forgot how furious she was with him and simply surrendered.

"Fine. Go." She checked the dainty watch on her wrist. "Five minutes."

Unexpectedly, he laughed. A harsh scrape of sound that shot from his throat like a bullet. "By God, you're the woman for me," he said, with a shake of his head. "You'll actually time me, won't you?"

"And am," she assured him. "Four and a half minutes now."

"Right then." He tossed back the rest of his wine and felt a lovely burn of fire in its wake. Setting the glass down, he forgot all about the words he'd practiced and blurted out, "When a man asks a woman to be his wife, he expects better than for her to turn on him like a snake."

She glanced at the watch again. "And when a woman hears a proposal, she sort of expects to hear something about 'love' in there somewhere."

This was the point that had chewed at him for three days. "And did your not-so-lamented Mike, ex-husband and all-around bastard, give you pretty words of love?"

Sean took a step closer and noted with some irritation that she stepped back. "Did he promise to be faithful, to love you always?"

A gleam of tears swamped her eyes and in the pale light, he watched as she ferociously blinked them back. "That was low."

"Aye, it was," he admitted, and cursed himself for the fool Ronan thought him to be. But at the same time, he bristled. "I didn't give you the words, but I gave you the promise. And I *keep* my promises. And if you weren't such a stubborn twit, you'd have realized that I wouldn't propose unless there were feelings there."

"Three and a half minutes," she announced, then added, "Even stubborn twits want to hear about those 'feelings' beyond 'I've a caring for you, Georgia.'"

He winced at the reminder of his own words. She'd given him "love"; he'd given her "caring." Maybe he was a fool. But that wasn't the point. "You should have known what I meant without me having to say it. Let me remind you again that your lying, miserable ex used the word *love* and it meant nothing."

"At least he had the courage to say it, even though his version of love was sadly lacking!"

Her eyes were hot balls of fury and perversely, Sean was as aroused by that as he was by everything else about her.

It tore at him, what she'd said. He *had* lacked the courage to say what he felt. But no more.

Pouring himself more wine, he took a long drink. "I won't be compared to a man who couldn't see you for the treasure you are, Georgia Page. In spite of your miserable temper and your stubbornness that makes a rock look agreeable in comparison."

"And I won't be told what I should do for 'my own

good.' Not by you and not by the villagers you've no doubt *paid* to sing your praises to me for the last three days."

"I didn't pay them!" He took a gulp of wine and set the glass down again. "That was our family's doing. I only found out about it tonight. Ailish and Laura sent Ronan off to do their bidding. He talked to Maeve, who then told every mother's son and daughter for miles to go to you with tales of my wondrousness." He glared at her. "For all the good that seems to have done.

"Besides," he added, "I've no need to bribe anyone because everyone else in my bloody life can plainly see what's in my heart without a bleeding *map!*"

"Yeah?" Georgia snapped with a glance at her watch. "Two minutes. Well, I do need a map. So tell me. Flat out, what *is* in your heart?"

"Love!" He threw both hands high and let them drop again. Irritated, frustrated beyond belief, he shouted it again. "Love! I love you. Have for weeks. Maybe longer," he mused, "but I can't be sure as you're turning me into a crazy man even as we're standing here!"

She smiled at him and his heart turned over.

"Oh, aye," he nodded grimly. "Now she smiles on me with benevolence, now that she's got me just where she wants me. Half mad with love and desire and the crushing worry that she'll walk away from me and leave me to go through the rest of my life without her scent flavoring my every breath. Without the taste of her lingering on my lips. Without the soft brush of her skin against mine. *This* she smiles for."

"Sean…"

"Rather than proposing, I should be committed. What I feel for you has destroyed my control. I feel so much for you, Georgia, it's all I can think of, dream of. I want to *marry* you. Make a family with you. Be your lover, your friend, the father of your children. Because I bloody well *love* you and if you can't see that, then too bloody bad because I won't be walking away from you. Ever."

"Sean…"

"I'm not the bloody clown you once pledged yourself to," he added, stabbing the air with his finger as he jabbed it at her. "You'll not compare me to him ever again."

"No," she said, still smiling.

"How much time have I left?"

"One minute," she said.

"Fine, then." He looked into those twilight eyes, and everything in him rushed toward the only happiness he would ever want or need. "Here it is, all laid out for you. I love you. And you bloody well love me. And you're damn well going to marry me at the first opportunity. And if you don't like that plan, you can spend the next fifty years complaining about it to me. But you *will* be mine. Make no mistake about that."

"You're nuts," Georgia said finally when the silence stretched out, humming with tension, with love, with the fraught emotions tangled up between them.

"I've said as much already, haven't I?"

"You have. And I love it."

He narrowed his gaze on her. "Is that right?"

"I do. I love everything about you, crazy man. I love how you look at me. I love that you think you can tell me what to do."

He scowled but, looking into her eyes, the dregs of his temper drained away, leaving him with only the love that had near choked him since the moment he'd first laid eyes on her.

"And I will marry you," she said, stepping into his arms. "On December twenty-second."

Gathering her up close, he asked, "Why the delay?"

"Because that way, Maeve wins the pool at the pub."

"You're a devious girl, Georgia," he said. "And perfect for me in every way."

"And don't you forget it," she said, grinning up at him.

"How much time have I got left?" he asked.

Never taking her gaze from his, she pulled her wristwatch off and tossed it aside. "We've got all the time in the world."

"That won't be enough," he whispered, and kissed her long and deep, until all the dark places inside him turned to blinding light.

Then he lifted his head and said softly, *"Tá tú an-an croí orm."*

She smiled and smoothed her fingertips across his cheek. "What does that mean?"

He kissed her fingers and told her, "'You're the very heart of me.'"

On a sigh, Georgia whispered, "Back atcha."

* * * * *

COMING NEXT MONTH from Harlequin Desire®
AVAILABLE NOVEMBER 27, 2012

#2197 ONE WINTER'S NIGHT

The Westmorelands

Brenda Jackson

Riley Westmoreland never mixes business with pleasure—until he meets his company's gorgeous new party planner and realizes one night will never be enough.

#2198 A GOLDEN BETRAYAL

The Highest Bidder

Barbara Dunlop

The head of a New York auction house is swept off her feet by the crown prince of a desert kingdom who has accused her of trafficking in stolen goods!

#2199 STAKING HIS CLAIM

Billionaires and Babies

Tessa Radley

She never planned a baby...he doesn't plan to let his baby go. The solution should be simple. But no one told Ella that love is the riskiest business of all....

#2200 BECOMING DANTE

The Dante Legacy

Day Leclaire

Gabe Moretti discovers he's not just a Moretti—he's a secret Dante. Now the burning passion—the Inferno—for Kat Malloy won't be ignored....

#2201 THE SHEIKH'S DESTINY

Desert Knights

Olivia Gates

Marrying Laylah is Rashid's means to the throne. But when she discovers his plot and casts him from her heart, will claiming the throne mean anything if he loses her?

#2202 THE DEEPER THE PASSION...

The Drummond Vow

Jennifer Lewis

When Vicki St. Cyr is forced to ask the man who broke her heart for help in claiming a reward, old passions and long-buried emotions flare.

You can find more information on upcoming Harlequin® titles, free excerpts and more at www.Harlequin.com.

HDCNM1112

REQUEST YOUR FREE BOOKS!
2 FREE NOVELS PLUS 2 FREE GIFTS!

Harlequin®

Desire

ALWAYS POWERFUL, PASSIONATE AND PROVOCATIVE

YES! Please send me 2 FREE Harlequin Desire® novels and my 2 FREE gifts (gifts are worth about $10). After receiving them, if I don't wish to receive any more books, I can return the shipping statement marked "cancel." If I don't cancel, I will receive 6 brand-new novels every month and be billed just $4.30 per book in the U.S. or $4.99 per book in Canada. That's a saving of at least 14% off the cover price! It's quite a bargain! Shipping and handling is just 50¢ per book in the U.S. and 75¢ per book in Canada.* I understand that accepting the 2 free books and gifts places me under no obligation to buy anything. I can always return a shipment and cancel at any time. Even if I never buy another book, the two free books and gifts are mine to keep forever.

225/326 HDN FEF3

Name _____ (PLEASE PRINT) _____

Address _____ Apt. # _____

City _____ State/Prov. _____ Zip/Postal Code _____

Signature (if under 18, a parent or guardian must sign)

Mail to the **Reader Service:**
IN U.S.A.: P.O. Box 1867, Buffalo, NY 14240-1867
IN CANADA: P.O. Box 609, Fort Erie, Ontario L2A 5X3

Not valid for current subscribers to Harlequin Desire books.

Want to try two free books from another line?
Call 1-800-873-8635 or visit www.ReaderService.com.

* Terms and prices subject to change without notice. Prices do not include applicable taxes. Sales tax applicable in N.Y. Canadian residents will be charged applicable taxes. Offer not valid in Quebec. This offer is limited to one order per household. All orders subject to credit approval. Credit or debit balances in a customer's account(s) may be offset by any other outstanding balance owed by or to the customer. Please allow 4 to 6 weeks for delivery. Offer available while quantities last.

Your Privacy—The Reader Service is committed to protecting your privacy. Our Privacy Policy is available online at www.ReaderService.com or upon request from the Reader Service.

We make a portion of our mailing list available to reputable third parties that offer products we believe may interest you. If you prefer that we not exchange your name with third parties, or if you wish to clarify or modify your communication preferences, please visit us at www.ReaderService.com/consumerschoice or write to us at Reader Service Preference Service, P.O. Box 9062, Buffalo, NY 14269. Include your complete name and address.

Harlequin® Desire is proud to present

ONE WINTER'S NIGHT

by New York Times *bestselling author*

Brenda Jackson

Alpha Blake tightened her coat around her. Not only would she be late for her appointment with Riley Westmoreland, but because of her flat tire they would have to change the location of the meeting and Mr. Westmoreland would be the one driving her there. This was totally embarrassing, when she had been trying to make a good impression.

She turned up the heat in her car. Even with a steady stream of hot air coming in through the car vents, she still felt cold, too cold, and wondered if she would ever get used to the Denver weather. Of course, it was too late to think about that now. It was her first winter here, and she didn't have any choice but to grin and bear it. When she'd moved, she'd felt that getting as far away from Daytona Beach as she could was essential to her peace of mind. But who in her right mind would prefer blistering-cold Denver to sunny Daytona Beach? Only a person wanting to start a new life and put a painful past behind her.

Her attention was snagged by an SUV that pulled off the road and parked in front of her. The door swung open and long denim-clad, boot-wearing legs appeared before a man stepped out of the truck. She met his gaze through the windshield and forgot to breathe. Walking toward her car was a man who was so dangerously masculine, so heart-stoppingly virile, that her brain went momentarily numb.

He was tall, and the Stetson on his head made him appear taller. But his height was secondary to the sharp handsomeness of his features.

Her gaze slid all over him as he moved his long limbs toward her vehicle in a walk that was so agile and self-assured, she envied the confidence he exuded with every step. Her breasts suddenly peaked, and she could actually feel blood rushing through her veins.

She didn't have to guess who this man was.

He was Riley Westmoreland.

Find out if Riley and Alpha mix business with pleasure in

ONE WINTER'S NIGHT

by Brenda Jackson

Available December 2012

Only from Harlequin® Desire

HARLEQUIN®

SPECIAL EDITION

Life, Love and Family

NEW YORK TIMES BESTSELLING AUTHOR

DIANA PALMER

brings you a brand-new Western romance
featuring characters that readers have come to
love—the Brannt family from Harlequin HQN's
bestselling book *WYOMING TOUGH*.

Cort Brannt, Texas rancher through and through,
is about to unexpectedly get lassoed by love!

THE RANCHER

Available November 13 wherever books are sold!

Also available as a 2-in-1
THE RANCHER & HEART OF STONE